# BRANDED

# BRANDED

L. E. EYRING

CITY OWL
PRESS

This book is a work of fiction. Names, characters, places, and incidents either are products of the author's imagination or are used fictitiously. Any resemblance to actual events or locales or persons, living or dead, is entirely coincidental and not intended by the author.

BRANDED
Demonic Tendencies, Book 1

CITY OWL PRESS
www.cityowlpress.com



Cover Design by MiblArt. All stock photos licensed appropriately.

Edited by Lisa Green.

For information on subsidiary rights, please contact the publisher at info@cityowlpress.com.

Paperback Edition ISBN: 978-1-64898-564-5

Digital Edition ISBN: 978-1-64898-565-2

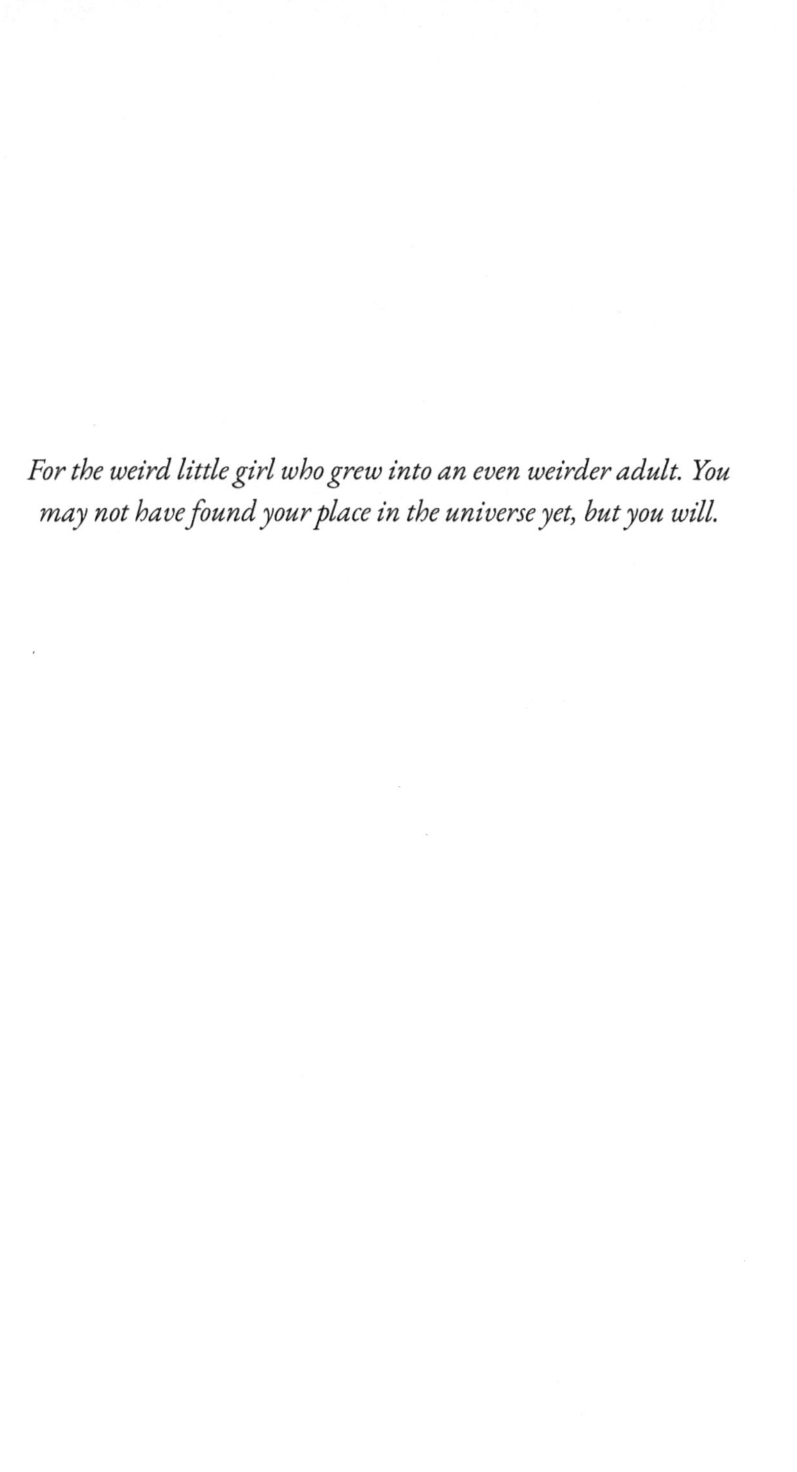

*For the weird little girl who grew into an even weirder adult. You may not have found your place in the universe yet, but you will.*

# PROLOGUE

He came into the world much the same way he did the first time: trembling, fearful, and wishing to return to the safe warmth of the womb.

Not that his escape route had been anything as natural as a birth canal, nor did Ash regret fleeing the place that was both an eternal nightmare and a living hell. But he'd forgotten what it meant to live. As if everything was designed to overload his senses—colors, smells and temperatures bombarding him from every angle until he wanted to scream. Perhaps all babies felt the same about their first push into existence.

But there were no hospitals or doctors here, and he was as far from a child as one could be. The room was dark, though his unnatural eyes could see as if it were bathed in brightness.

A bedroom, one meant for a child with its posters of dinosaurs and far-off galaxies. A little boy's room, he thought, until he spotted the child huddled against the closed door.

Huddled, because other things had escaped alongside Ash. They soared out of the open window, squirmed into the cracks in the wallpaper, or wriggled into the shadowed corners. Ash himself had retreated to the first shelter he could find—the metal-frame bed pushed against the wall.

The girl, somewhere around the age of ten and old enough to know better, approached his hiding place. Him, with all his twisted and grotesque and no longer recognizable parts. A real monster under the bed.

She must have seen his violent arrival through the opening between worlds, yet she didn't cry, or scream, or run. She crept forward, careful but calm, and peeked under the bed. She held out something, like a peace offering. A stuffed toy. A little gray tabby cat.

With nails too long and sharp, Ash accepted the toy with great care. This was something undoubtedly precious to her, meant to bring him comfort. A way to show that she understood what it was to be afraid, and that he wasn't alone.

And he held the gift close to his heart, unaware that with the gesture, he damned them both.

## CHAPTER ONE

# SAM

It was late, and Sam was a little drunk.

Her head pounded to the rhythm of her heart, and her feet ached to the same tune. The taxi driver had been silent the entire ride, and even with dubious glances in the rearview mirror, she appreciated his professional, not-my-business policy.

She tossed her purse on the counter and pulled off her scuffed boots. Loud wailing announced itself from the kitchen doorway.

"Hey, little man." Sam bent to pet the large cat as he skittered around her, dancing away when she attempted to stroke his back. "Hungry?"

Monster screamed his affirmation. Sam stepped around him and put down a can without mishap, which was a miracle considering her next stumble down the hallway. She weaved through the bathroom door and flipped on the light, startling herself with her reflection.

Pale skin, fetid wounds, and copious amounts of blood and exposed bone stared back. Crimson oozed from the right corner of her mouth, her eyes hollow with a dead light, her skin as colorless as a grave.

Office socials weren't usually her thing, but a Halloween party with her coworkers dressed up in equally silly costumes sounded fun. And it had been—until Davin left the party with his arm wrapped around Theresa's shoulders.

*Traitor.* Not once had Sam expressed interest in the party, but after this morning when Theresa popped her head into Sam's cubicle and encouraged her to go because *a certain someone would be there,* Sam had thought...

Well, it didn't matter what she'd thought. Sam's crush had reached a dead end, which was fine. She wasn't bothered. The hollowness in her eyes was just another piece of fictitious costume.

At least Sam had washed down the bitter taste with an open bar.

She disassembled the zombie ensemble one wretched piece at a time, washed the stage makeup from her face, and picked the black glitter and fake blood from her yellow hair, but left on the ghoulish nail polish. A little souvenir wouldn't hurt. No one paid attention to her hands.

Sam stayed under the hot shower spray just long enough to scrub clean the cadaver blush, then made it to bed with an undead shuffle. She was getting too sober, and after pulling on a loose Alice Cooper shirt and a pair of red flannel pants, she crawled under the covers.

She waited. And waited. And sleep wouldn't come.

Disappointment wouldn't relinquish its grip, nor would the image of what her coworkers might be doing at that moment. Her stomach twisted, and she turned on her side to glare at the sterile apartment walls rather than her popcorn-textured ceiling.

Halloween used to belong to her and her father, and now it

was hers alone. It was supposed to be *her* night, and all Sam wanted to do was go to sleep and pretend it hadn't happened.

Monster leapt onto the bed and wailed at her lack of adoration. She shushed him, which he ignored and wailed again. Her neighbors would love that.

Sam thought of Mr. Morris scowling at their shared wall, and she smiled and stroked the cat's fur. Monster curled against her side and began his nightly ritual of bathing and choking on his own hairballs.

The comforting rattle of a happy cat eased her to sleep.

A growl and a heavy weight on her chest wrenched her awake.

Sam stared at the ceiling, unable to draw a full breath. She tried to lift her arms and head, but they didn't respond. Her hands and feet were just as inert.

The growl rose into a warning hiss, then an angry yowl. Monster's weight shifted and his fur puffed as he faced something next to her.

Blood roaring through her ears, her fingers trembling but immovable, Sam's body became a stranger. Adrenaline tangled her panicked thoughts as she tried to draw a deep breath that wouldn't come.

In, out, in, and out came her too-slow breathing. She was going to suffocate, unable to get enough oxygen to her racing heart.

Her body was a useless thing, except for her eyes, and her gaze skittered across the room like a camera operator on too much stimulant. A shadow loomed in the corner of her vision, and she focused on the dark shape as it drew closer. It stared back.

She drew a breath to scream, and it died a faint, rasping death.

Monster growled again, and the shadow turned its attention on him. Its eyes were venomous green with a faded glow, barely visible in the dark. Its face was smooth, featureless aside from the eyes, until it changed. Folds of skin peeled away from where its mouth and nose should be, and its face opened like a poisonous flower transforming into a gaping mouth lined with rows and rows of triangular teeth.

*Like a shark,* Sam thought, until she saw the teeth continue all the way to its throat, undulating with flexible, crushing muscle.

It leaned forward, angling its petal-like maw over her face. Its breath washed over her, foul and rancid, and her gag reflex threatened to kick in. If she vomited now, she would choke on it.

The edges of its mouth covered her vision until she could no longer see her room. Sam was going to die in her bed, and no one would know what really killed her. She squeezed her eyes shut, like a child who pretended the monster wasn't there if she couldn't see it, but she whimpered. A small animal noise, one she was certain would be the last one she would ever make.

A sharp yowl startled Sam. She opened her eyes, and the creature flinched backwards. Claw marks oozed across its forehead, and something black dripped down its face. Monster had never so much as bullied a spider, yet he raked again at the creature's eyes and barely missed the rows of hungry teeth.

The creature emitted a deep, rumbling moan, like the song of a whale being dragged into an abyss. It echoed in the hollows of Sam's chest and vibrated along her bones.

It raised a clawed hand, curved and wicked. Sam fought the invisible weight of her paralysis, attempting to open her mouth to scream. Her jaw remained locked tight.

If the creature ripped her apart, so be it, but not Monster. Not him. He didn't deserve this. *He didn't—*

The wooden frame of her window gave a violent crack and burst apart; the lock shattered as the pane of glass jammed upward, sticking in place. A gust of cold wind howled into the bedroom, tugging at Sam's hair and loose bedsheets.

The shadow hesitated, claws frozen in midair. It gave another rumbling moan that made Sam think of deep places in the earth where humans had never reached.

There was a loud, rushing *snap,* as if someone was shaking out a pair of thick sheets, and once the sound vanished, the air went still. Something else loomed in the dark, but she couldn't turn her head to see what new horror had arrived.

The creature looming over her retreated from sight. Monster no longer yowled, his anger reduced to a faint growl.

A voice spoke. It was...a man, though he spoke a language she didn't know. The words twisted and slithered, spat and curled around vowels and consonants, and the hairs on Sam's body stood upright.

The creature responded, moaning another dying-whale noise that would haunt Sam's nightmares if she lived through the current one.

The second intruder answered with sharp irritation easily recognizable across any language.

Another moan, this one sounding argumentative, if a moan could be such a thing. Whatever the creature was unhappy about, its response was cut short.

With a brilliant flash of light and a furious *crack* that split the air, the room fell silent, and a rotten smell filled Sam's nostrils. She gagged, cut off from the already meager supply of air as her unwilling throat refused to open.

She shut her eyes tight and focused on trying to breathe, but panic, combined with the stench of rotten eggs, pushed her too far. Sam choked, and tears sprang at the corners of her eyes. She'd never wanted to breathe so badly, and her body revolted at being denied.

Something touched the base of her throat, and like a valve opening a floodgate, she breathed.

Sam sucked in as much oxygen as she could, greedy for blessed, life-giving air, even if it reeked of something noxious. But strangely, it didn't. Instead, it was rich and earthy with a hint of pine, as if Sam had been dropped in the middle of a forest, or the forest had been brought to her. There was something about it that tugged at the corner of her mind, but she was too thankful to breathe to care.

Whatever had touched her throat was gone. She tried to turn her head, but her neck muscles were stiff and uncooperative. She groaned in frustration, surprised she could make the sound. The sleep paralysis must be wearing off, and she would fully awaken soon.

That's all it was, some kind of sleep-induced hallucination. Except Monster was still perched on her chest, and he never sat on her, not even on her lap during movie nights.

There was a touch on Sam's temple, so light she questioned whether it was there. Then it happened again, tracing across her skin, unmistakably real.

She jerked her head away. Her heart sped up in a frantic beat, but adrenaline did nothing to break her out of the paralysis. She was helpless. Down, down, the touch continued, following the pulse point of Sam's throat to her collarbone. It stopped there—it had to—Monster was occupying the space and seemed intent on not moving. He was also no longer growling.

*"Pax,"* the man murmured.

Her cat—who didn't like anyone and barely tolerated Sam herself—purred.

Muscles sluggish and strained, Sam tilted her head downward.

The man wasn't quite a man. His dark hair reached his shoulders, framing eyes that held no color or warmth. Twin horns curved back from his temples, gray and textured like they belonged to something in the gazelle family. His fingernails were sharp, his ears tapered, and though he kept his mouth firmly closed, Sam imagined sharp teeth hiding from view.

On the back of his left hand was some kind of symbolic tattoo. Or maybe tattoo wasn't the right word since the lines looked like they had been carved into his flesh with an uncaring knife.

The man moved his hand out of view, and that drew her attention to something else behind him—large, dark, and folded behind his back. Even more surreal than the horns, and the maybe-wings, and the quite-possible-tail flicking behind him, was the fact he was stroking Monster's fur.

*"Reliquam,"* the stranger said. Not to Sam—to her cat. *"Tutum est."*

Monster stood on all fours and stretched. Sam wheezed as his considerable weight pressed on her sternum. He sauntered to the edge of the bed and leapt down, then she could no longer see him.

Sam's cat had left her alone with a demon.

The demon in question stared at her. His eyes weren't colorless, not entirely. Just an unnerving gray that seemed unable to hold anything other than cold watchfulness.

For a demon, his clothes were surprisingly pedestrian: a white tank top and gray sweatpants, as if he'd just rolled out of bed. His bare shoulders revealed the smooth muscles of his arms, continuing into the dip of his neckline. When he shifted, the wings appeared weighty, and she wondered if they were heavy. It would explain his massive chest, the size of which would make any gym rat envious.

When he reached toward her face, she flinched. The movement was tiny, barely anything within the paralytic hold on her body, but the demon paused, his hand inches from her cheek.

The next words he spoke, she understood.

"I won't hurt you."

His voice was low and calm, almost soothing, but that didn't mean she wanted him touching her.

"As I told your hobgoblin," he continued, "you're safe now."

Sam's tongue unglued from her soft palate, and she wet her chapped lips. "My...what?"

Instead of answering, the demon reached forward and brushed the side of her jaw. His fingers slid downward across her neck to rest on her collarbone, the touch strange along her skin. It didn't hurt, but it didn't feel great, like the pins-and-needles of blood returning to a sleeping limb.

Sam couldn't have moved even without the paralysis. *What the hell was he doing?*

"You need to relax," he muttered, as if she were the problem. "The *Alp's* venom is still in your system. It'll take a few minutes to wear off. Touch helps speed up the process."

*Venom? Alp?*

"That...that thing...with the teeth?" Sam's own teeth clattered against each other, the twitch of her muscles causing involuntary spasms.

The demon had moved on, running both of his hands down her arms. It *did* help return blood flow to her body; it did *not* disquiet the growing cacophony in Sam's head.

"Yeah, and it's a real bastard too," he said. "They're not typically bold like this, feeding in the middle of a populated area."

Sam didn't have much to say to that, nor did she know how to handle his conversational tone, so she asked the first thing that came to mind. "Are you a demon?"

His face remained blank in a way that seemed constructed, and he said, "For the most part."

"I'm going to need a little more than that."

He snorted through his nose.

Sam frowned.

"I wasn't always—" His hands moved down her stomach, tickling as the tips of his nails scraped along sensitive skin. "I used to be human once. A long time ago."

Sam caught the scent again. Pine and earth, like a deep, dark wood. It had no business being so familiar, evoking memories of old campgrounds, pitched tents, and the tangy flavor of a smoldering campfire. A distant part of Sam knew she should be having the nervous breakdown of a lifetime, but that part was pleasantly numb and disconnected.

*I'm dissociating,* Sam thought. She'd been doing so well, too.

The weight of hands brought her back, resting on the curve of Sam's hips with thumbs pressed into the sliver of skin between her shirt and pants. His expression was uninterested, clinical, as if he didn't quite notice or care what part of her he focused on.

Sam did. She certainly did.

"What's your name?"

The demon took a slow, deep breath and expelled it with far more heaviness than the question warranted. "You're kidding me."

Sam frowned again.

"I can't move, I think I was just attacked, and your hands are all over me—"

"Ash."

She stared. "As in ash from a fire?"

The demon formed a pinched look that said he questioned her intelligence. "It's short for Ashley, which happens to be my name. Ashley Kane Spiros. And before you ask, it's Greek."

Sam closed her mouth, and the edges of her lips trembled. "What do you want with me?"

He gave her another dubious look and said, "You? Nothing. Except maybe to stop acting like demon bait."

"What?"

"Did you think this was your first time?"

There was a faint smile there, but it was curled with a bitter flavor. His eyes met hers, dark pools that chilled the room a few degrees. His hands rested on her thighs before traveling to her knees. With the revelation of his name, ordinarily human, she'd forgotten the paralysis of her legs.

"I'll tell you a story about a silly little girl," he began. "This silly little girl decides one day to play with one of those...what are they called? Ouija boards?"

*No.*

"A toy for kids, one you can buy at any big box store. It's not supposed to actually do anything, but with a focused intent and being at the right place at the right time? Stranger things have happened."

*No, that's not—*

"Let's say, something unfortunate did happen. A girl like that wouldn't be particularly smart, opening a portal to another realm and releasing monsters into her world." He shrugged with one shoulder, something rustling on his back. "Not smart at all. Can't say her luck has improved in twenty-five years."

"Nothing happened," Sam whispered. Her palms were slick,

and cold sweat dotted her skin. "I remember the Ouija board, but that's it. That's *it.* Nothing happened."

The demon's lips split into a smile filled with pearly white teeth. Some of them were pointed. Sam hated being right.

"You don't remember, because I didn't want you to remember." The smile vanished, and his jaw clenched with the force of a bite. "That sort of thing can ruin someone, break their minds in a way that can't be fixed. I didn't want that for you."

Her voice was faint and very far away. "You were there."

The demon's hands curled over her feet, rubbing the last of the paralysis from her soles. Sam barely felt it.

"I was there, because you freed me." His expression was grim, and his eyes were the color of tombstones. "You've had a lot of nasty stuff following you over the years, Samara. You have no idea what I've protected you from."

CHAPTER TWO

# SAM

THE ROOM WAS TOO BRIGHT.

Sam closed her eyes and rolled over. The blackout curtain must have fallen again. Damn thing got unstuck at the worst times, and since she wasn't allowed to put holes in the apartment walls, she had to use tape to fix it back over the windows.

Usually, they unstuck when the room was too warm and the tape lost its adhesion, but Sam was cold, and when she adjusted her position, she realized why.

She realized a couple of things, actually. One, she felt like she'd been hit by a truck and every inch of her hurt, and two, every inch of her was also naked.

That got her eyes open, albeit squinting as she winced into a sitting position. Her sleep clothes were tossed on the floor in a careless spread, and her skin was covered in scratches and bruises.

Something itched at the back of her mind. Something important and too large to grasp, and her heart raced. She couldn't breathe. She tucked her legs against her chest and braced her forehead on her knees, focused on breathing in and out.

*It wasn't real,* she repeated mentally, unsure of what she was denying but firm that she should deny it. *Not real, not real. Can't be real. Wasn't real.*

She clawed at her memories like they were a life jacket and she was slipping under dark waters. What could she remember? Coming home, taking off the ghoulish makeup, and then...what? Another night terror. It had been a long time since an episode, and nothing so vivid and detailed. The memory of the cloying stench had her rubbing the front of her neck.

And then...someone woke her. Some random guy who had gone overboard with the gargoyle aesthetics. Had she met him at the party? She couldn't remember bringing him home, or letting him in, or why the hell she would—

A yowl interrupted the thoughts ricocheting around her skull. Monster waited at the door to her bedroom, and when she didn't respond beyond a motionless, slack-jawed stare, he sauntered over and leapt onto the bed.

"Hobgoblin," Sam murmured.

Monster continued his vigil, waiting for her crisis to pass so she could get on with breakfast. She reached out to pet him—and then stopped. She stared at her hand, and unfortunately, blinking didn't make what she saw go away.

On the back of her hand lay a faint red symbol, etched into her skin.

*What the fuck?*

Thin lines curved in crescents with tips that didn't quite meet, intersecting each other in nothing familiar or recognizable. The symbol was perfectly even, sketched with the quality of a surgeon's hand, and Sam had no recollection of how it had gotten there.

She covered her face with her hands. What had she done? Gotten so black out drunk that she'd taken a stranger home, had sex with him, and then let him give her a homemade stick and poke? *Hah.*

There was another explanation that soured her mouth and tightened her stomach. She didn't think she'd been that drunk when she came home, nor did she remember anyone being in the taxi with her. She may have been drugged and followed home.

She shivered and curled into a tighter ball. Should she call the police?

*No.* Sam wasn't sure what was real and what wasn't, nor did she know if there was anything to report.

Funnily enough, it was Monster that made her doubt her own memories. The large cat waited patiently next to her legs, sitting on his haunches and staring at her with lidded eyes. A cat perfectly at ease. The few times she'd had a friend visit, Monster wouldn't even let them into the apartment without hissing and yowling—Sam couldn't imagine a stranger in her bedroom without Monster having a tantrum.

But he seemed happy, content, and faintly mocking in that way all satisfied felines were.

She had a few minutes before she needed to get up, but Sam turned off her phone alarm, slipped on an oversized shirt and headed to the kitchen to feed the beast. Everything else appeared normal in her apartment, and Sam would have relaxed if she hadn't stepped into the bathroom.

In her pale reflection, a circular row of teeth marks marred the skin between her shoulder and neck, four points deep enough to have broken the skin. If there had been blood, someone had wiped it clean.

There was little evidence of her sexual encounter, either. He must have cleaned her up or used condoms, if sex had happened at all.

It had. Even if there wasn't a deep ache in her pelvis and her thighs weren't sore as if she'd run a marathon, waking up naked would be suspicious enough. Sam couldn't sleep unless she was covered head to toe and wrapped in too many blankets. Plus, it was autumn in Seattle, and she didn't have the money to waste on heat.

When glaring at her reflection yielded no answers, she took a thorough shower that felt more like decontamination than washing. Afterwards, she yanked on her dark pantsuit and untangled her hair, no mercy spared for buttons or brush. Sam might not remember the details, but she had a place to start: a name that repeated itself, attached to a face that wouldn't stay in focus.

*Ashley Kane Spiros.*

---

SAM WAS EXHAUSTED down to her bones, and it would have been so much easier to call in sick. Hell, she *felt* sick. But if she stayed home, she would lie in bed, stare at the ceiling, and try her best not to think—which would only make her think more.

At least at work, she wouldn't be alone. Even the quiet company in neighboring cubicles was enticing compared to the silence that awaited her in her apartment, punctuated only by Monster's demands that could be resolved or ignored.

After filling her thermos with coffee from the pot and dragging herself to her car, Sam fought through morning traffic to arrive at her office building. The gray November sky made the water of the Puget Sound equally dull. Normally she would enjoy a view like this, but nothing felt *normal,* not even her regular routine. She found a free parking space in the underground garage, dug the keycard lanyard out of her bag and slipped it over her head, left her car, and headed to the elevators. She swiped her keycard over the reader and the elevator was summoned, just as it was every day.

Easy. Routine. And completely surreal.

Sam didn't know what she expected. Some sign that perhaps the world was different to match her own internal wrongness.

But everything in the office was the same, all evidence of the previous night's party cleaned and swept away. The drab, poorly ventilated breakroom. The sad kitchenette with faded, eggshell tile walls. The harsh, fluorescent lights over the rows of cubicles, and the monochromatic gray carpet as a finishing flourish. They were all typical standard for an office building, a constant reminder to its employees that they couldn't escape gray scale no matter where they looked.

Today, that soulless, corporate aesthetic was almost comforting in its familiarity. Nothing bad happened here. Everything was the same, and there were no concerning memories of rows of sharp teeth, or the warmth of a tongue running over her neck.

Sam was breathing hard again. Head down, eyes open but unseeing, she bumped into something solid, and hands gripped her arms to steady her. When she looked up, ready to apologize, her stomach sank.

"Hey, Wandern," Davin greeted her with a smile. Her lack of response didn't curb his cheer, her own personal sun that would force her to bask in his presence. "How are you? You look tired."

"Fine. I'm fine."

His hands were still on her shoulders, the weight of them heavy, while he remained oblivious.

"Yeah? That's good."

She waited, and finally, he let her go.

"You get home okay last night?" he asked with another friendly smile.

Sam shifted the strap of her bag. "Yeah. Why wouldn't I?"

Her suspicious tone was like a tennis ball against a brick building, unnoticed and deflected.

"You had some drinks at the party, right? I wondered if you caught a ride with anyone." He shrugged as if it made no difference to him, and yet he still stood there. Talking. In fact, he was blocking Sam's cubicle.

"Uh, yeah. I mean, no." She winced. "I took a taxi. Stacey called one for me."

Having her boss call a taxi had been embarrassing enough, but since she'd carpooled to the party with Theresa, Sam hadn't had much choice about her ride home.

Sam shifted again, hoping he would take it as a sign to move out of the way, but a small part of her, the part that still smarted at how he'd ignored her at the Halloween party, urged her to speak. "You and Theresa have fun?"

Davin's brows rose.

*Yeah,* Sam thought, *I noticed.*

"Eh, not really." He rubbed a hand through his dirty blond hair, ruffling the strands into a messier configuration. "We hung for a while, but that was it. I tried to look for you afterwards, but when I couldn't find you, I figured you'd left."

Sam stared. He'd looked for her. That was...unlikely. More likely, Davin and Theresa had fucked, he'd gotten bored, and then he'd left her there without a second glance. Maybe Sam had dodged a bullet.

"Anyway," Davin cleared his throat, breaking the silence that

Sam let linger between them. "You sure you're all right? Nothing happened after the party?"

Now *that* got her attention. She studied his face, but there was only a vague look of concern.

Her muscles relaxed by the smallest degree. Davin didn't know. He couldn't. She was paranoid and jumpy, and Davin might be a little bit of a slut, but he didn't have anything to do with what happened last night.

"I'm okay. Thanks."

Sam semi-forced him out of the way as she dropped her bag onto her desk. She was happy to move on from this conversation, but Davin lingered behind her. She took a breath, pulled a tight smile that hurt at the corners, and glanced over her shoulder to add, "I have lots of work to get done before the weekend, so..."

"Right. Course."

He gave a sheepish smile, the dangerous kind with perfect white teeth and warm green eyes. The kind of smile that would have frozen her like a spooked animal before. Now, she gave him a dull expression that followed him around the corner as he disappeared from sight, blocked by the slate-gray fabric of the cubicle walls.

Sam sat at her desk, powered on her computer, and sorted out her plan for the day: *Do not think about anything outside of requisition forms and medical supply fulfillment.*

Pulling up her inbox, Sam started with the emails, going through what she'd missed from the morning announcements: a handful of meetings that didn't involve her department, an alert to join a new company-wide app encouraging employees to participate in a more "healthy and active lifestyle!", and another fake phishing email that was entrapment courtesy of the IT department.

She quickly deleted them all and dove into the bulk of her work, double-checking fill requests, calling clients for the complicated cases, and ensuring vendors had enough supply on hand to meet the demands of their clients.

It was tedious, mundane, soul-crushing work, but today, Sam was grateful for the distraction. It wasn't a bad job. It kept the bills paid, barely covered the exorbitant Seattle rental costs, and ensured Monster had four square meals a day. Five, if he was greedy and Sam was feeling weak-willed.

Still, after a short time, Sam's mind wandered into dangerous territory, once again trying to pierce through the heavy mental fog that clouded last night's events. It remained opaque, except for a tiny glimpse. Not so much a look as it was a feeling: a faint pressure between her thighs.

Sam stood so fast she banged her legs on the desk. She ignored the sting as she retreated to the breakroom. A pot of coffee was already brewing, and she inhaled the rich smell, but the comfort was fleeting. Even the buzz of caffeine couldn't keep her focused on spreadsheets and forms once she returned to her desk.

On top of her anxiety about the previous night, Sam's thoughts kept returning to this morning. There were things about Monster that made him weird, even for a cat. He seemed to know when she was getting sick or when fatigue was about to hit her. She'd joked more than once that he was her therapy animal, but he really was. Warm, comforting, reliable, but with everyone else, he was strange and prickly. Even her mom called him creepy the few times she'd visited from Spokane. Her mom said the way the light shimmered off his pupils was unnatural and that he seemed more demon than feline.

*Part-cat, part-demon.*

Sam's fingers were motionless on the keyboard and had been for some time.

Leaning back in her chair, she peered around the edge of her worker pen. No one paid attention. Everyone else was bent over their own workstations or mindlessly thumbing through their phones. She scooted close to her desk, closed down her work, and opened an internet browser.

An hour later, Sam was still clicking through pages, scouring them. She nearly forgot she was supposed to be working. Hobgoblins, according to most websites, were helpful spirits that resembled small, hairy men. On a few occasions, Sam had referred to Monster as a "little man" because it was funny, not because it was accurate.

She searched another word, one that had floated in the back of her thoughts, and ultimately, Sam thought it would turn out nothing except searches on alpine trees.

She was wrong.

*Alpen* originated from German folklore and were known to attack victims in their sleep, creating nightmares from their dreams. They sat on the chests of their victims, weighing them down so they couldn't breathe. The *Alp* appeared as a squat, elf-like creature wearing a conical hat, and looked more like a garden gnome than a monstrous shape in the dark.

Sam relaxed until she reached the bottom of the page where a single link stood out in the search engine.

*The* Alpen, *in many cases, are considered to be demons...*

Heat coiled up her face and settled in her cheeks. Someone was fucking with her. Implanting the idea that she'd been attacked by a demon, when in reality, she was the target of a cruel joke.

Heart thundering and nausea tightening the back of her

throat, she opened a new browser. Maybe she wouldn't find anything, but anyone stupid enough to get her drunk and tattoo her might be stupid enough to give her his real name.

She didn't expect any hits. She got three.

Each article she opened pulled an imaginary band tighter around her chest. Each article said the same thing, equally sparse in detail and comfort.

In 1971, a high school science teacher from the small town of Aspen Falls, Arizona, went missing. The teacher was never found and was eventually declared dead *in absentia* by his fiancée. He was survived by her, his parents, and a younger sister.

The man smiling from the faculty photo had short hair and round glasses, but there was no mistaking the slope of his nose, the full angle of his jaw, or those somber, gray eyes.

Sam had a one-night stand with a teacher who went missing fifty years ago, and he hadn't aged a day.

## CHAPTER THREE

# SAM

The days passed, each bringing with it less of an expectation that Ashley Kane Spiros, or someone committing extremely convincing identity theft, would appear to upend her life a second time.

She'd printed out everything she could find and kept it in a manila folder on her coffee table. Every night, without fail, she took out the pages and read them again, looking for something she had missed. Sam would call it a hobby, in the way one might call picking a scab or tonguing a sore tooth a hobby.

Work was a poor distraction, the repetition of vendor requests and bulk inventory invoices not enough to keep her mind occupied. In fact, almost everything about her life was the same, which made the disjointed pieces even more out of place, all wrong angles and corners that would no longer slot together.

There were two things that served as a continuous reminder: the red symbol that wouldn't go away no matter how raw she scrubbed her skin, and Davin.

She couldn't figure him out. Every opportunity he had to flag Sam's attention, whether in the breakroom, the parking lot, or even her cubicle, he did so. Stranger still was the way he completely ignored Theresa, and that Theresa seemed to be ignoring him too.

Theresa, bubbly and chipper and constantly making conversation with her cubicle neighbors, now kept to herself. She'd called in sick the day after the party and still looked unwell. She had bags under her eyes and a hollowness to her cheeks, and her previous bouncy energy had vanished.

In fact, she looked a lot like Sam felt.

Sam wished she were a better person, the kind who would ask Theresa how she was doing, but Sam had her own problems, and with each passing week...they grew worse.

At first, Sam ignored it.

The second week, she told herself it would pass.

The third week, Sam knew something was wrong.

By the fourth week, Sam was in pain and terrified.

She stood in front of the mirror, having waited until the women's restroom at work was empty before pulling off her fingerless gloves.

The symbol, no longer a faint pink color, was wet and crimson, as if her hand was filled with blood that threatened to spill over. The skin around the ink lines was angry and inflamed, tender and hot when she touched it. She'd done enough ill-advised medical searches to know what an infected tattoo looked like, but the pain was something else. From irritation to itch, now it seared into her skin as if she were being scorched to the bone.

Pulling paper towels out of the dispenser, Sam wet the sheets with cool water and pressed them to the mark. The water was ice cold on her burning skin, providing some relief.

Sam couldn't wait any longer. Doctor's offices would be shut down over the holiday weekend, and waiting in the ER wasn't how she wanted to spend her Thanksgiving.

The clinic was packed when Sam arrived after work, but when she showed the receiving nurse the infected tattoo, they put her on the list for urgent cases. Even though her time in the waiting room was brief, Sam tried to make herself smaller. She closed her eyes, but she swore she could feel the other patients looking at her, judging her, sensing something was deeply wrong with her.

Sam couldn't disagree with them.

After the nurse took her vitals and announced that she had a mild fever, Sam swallowed her pride and asked for additional tests. The doctor gave her antibiotics through an IV line and told her if symptoms didn't improve within twenty-four hours, she must go to the emergency room.

Right. Sepsis. At least she didn't have to worry about chlamydia, gonorrhea, or being pregnant, or so the nurse informed her. After the IV bag was drained of the saline cocktail, she was given a prescription for antibiotics and released.

The drive home was hell. Her hand throbbed in time with her heartbeat, pulsing fire across her skin in the shape of the symbol. Fear tightened her throat; she might not have a choice about the hospital.

Just one more day. One day to let the antibiotics work and prove it was nothing more than a wound infection.

Rain splattered the windshield, making it hard to see the nighttime traffic. It was the kind of weather that made Sam want to be at home sipping hot cocoa on the couch with Monster curled at her feet.

Instead, she stopped at a local doughnut shop and picked up a variety box of four, all vegan with cutesy, weird autumnal themes.

One particular design drew her eye: a chocolate doughnut with red frosting detailing the lines of a pentagram across its surface.

Sam did not include that one in her assortment.

It had been a while since she treated herself, and even though she felt like she was being cooked from the inside out, she wanted to celebrate the fact she was clean and not pregnant.

She didn't feel clean, and Sam gripped the steering wheel tight. No matter how much she tried to pass off Halloween night as a drunken escapade, it wasn't how she felt. There had been fear —yes, lots of that—but not of the man himself. And that was something she couldn't explain.

Random pieces of information would float into her thoughts like errant soap bubbles. First, the words hobgoblin and *Alp* wouldn't go away until she found out what they meant. And then she kept thinking of the Ouija board she'd played with soon after she turned ten, an age where she should have started to move on from such childish toys. Still, most kids messed with those things with no ill effects, as far as she knew. So why the fixation?

And then...she would get flashes of touching him, and of him touching her. She thought they had been talking about something, and then it all went dark. She might not remember what happened afterwards, but she could feel a warm body pressed to hers. *His* warm body.

The fucked-up memories were responsible for her other problem, she was sure of it. Sam's sex drive rarely left neutral, but with confusing images and phantom touches growing more and more insistent, the gear was being forced into forward acceleration.

Sam turned on the AC even though it was in the low fifties outside, but each bump in the road made her legs clench tighter.

Thankfully, she soon pulled into her designated spot, turned off the ignition, and climbed out of her car.

The cool air and drizzling rain were soothing on her hot skin, but the relief was temporary. As soon as she entered her apartment complex, the warmth inside weighed heavily on her skin, and her hand flared hot in a steady tempo.

*Tomorrow. I'll go to the hospital tomorrow.*

As soon as she got inside her apartment, she planned to strip down and take a cold shower. Turning off the heat might also help her fever. It was fortunate her only roommate had fur and couldn't linguistically complain.

Sam's keys jingled as she worked the key into the lock. She expected the sound of excited meows, but only silence greeted her.

She turned the knob as if it were a live grenade and tipped the door open with her shoulder. The dark apartment welcomed her with the same still quiet. The hair on her neck tingled, and she clenched her keys between her knuckles as she nudged the door shut behind her.

The smart thing would have been to leave, go to a neighboring apartment, and tell them she might have an intruder, but she didn't have any proof. Just an absent cat, and she wouldn't leave without knowing if Monster was okay.

She was wrong; it wasn't completely dark. A soft glow illuminated the living room, but Sam always turned off her lights before leaving for work.

She walked into the living room at a slow, dreamlike pace. She willed herself to see nothing, but the scene before her was inevitable, like a child checking her closet for monsters and finding one inside.

Sitting on the couch, knees spread wide as if she were the intruder and this was his domain, sat Ashley Kane Spiros.

He didn't look like he did in the old newspaper articles or the faculty pictures. He didn't look human at all. Horns swept back from the sides of his head; large, webbed wings tucked behind his back; and a tail draped over the couch cushions like a sleeping snake.

The blurry memories of someone in her room, waking up with bruises and a freshly inked tattoo, the heavy feeling on the back of her neck of things unremembered in her mind but faintly recalled by her body—those were things she could accept.

This was not.

He held something in his hands, a stack of papers, removed from their folder. The papers she'd printed with everything she could find on the missing teacher. He was reading them. *Had* been reading them. Now he glared up at her, pupils glinting like the eyes of a nocturnal animal.

The creature who looked like Ashley Kane Spiros, unmistakable even with his longer hair and distinct lack of aging, tossed the papers down on the coffee table, his mouth twisted in a frown. Her tattoo flared hot, as if she'd done something worthy of punishment.

*He's real. I didn't imagine it. He's here. He's real.*

The demon leaned forward, braced his elbows on his knees, and spoke. "What the hell is *this?*"

## CHAPTER FOUR

# ASH

<u>HALLOWEEN NIGHT</u>

Ash was lucky he didn't have anything breakable on his rooftop because the speed with which he landed would have sent any chairs or tables spiraling across the deck.

When his shoes met the balcony, he nearly collapsed to his knees from the lack of strength in his legs. His progress to the landing and down the staircase was clumsy, but hey, at least he didn't have to worry about a broken neck.

The clock tower was as dark as he'd left it, bathed in shadow and faint moonlight, but Ash didn't turn on the lights. He went straight to the kitchen and filled a glass in the sink, water spilling over his fingers. His hand trembled, and he couldn't get it to stop. He couldn't fill his lungs, and a dreadful weight filled his bones as if someone had replaced the marrow with lead.

Ash hadn't meant for it to happen. Didn't know how the fuck it *could* happen. He'd wiped memories before, too numerous to count, and none of them had misfired. Not like this.

Ash drained the glass, as if the desperate deluge could cleanse him of his actions. His stomach ached, but he ignored it. The demon part of him was sluggish and satisfied, and why wouldn't it be? It had gorged itself, and he'd felt like an overfed mosquito, swaying drunkenly on the biting wind all the way home.

The intensity of it, the raw, consuming hunger and blissful satisfaction that came after—Ash would take it all back if he could. His stomach churned as the saliva soured in his mouth, but the thing of it was...Ash didn't know what he could have done differently.

He'd been right to go to Samara. The *Alp* had been in her bedroom, had paralyzed her, poised to feed like the foul leech it was. And then it had the audacity to argue with him, stating that if it fed first, Ash could feast on the *leftovers.*

Ash had disavowed him of that notion by sending him straight back to Hell, or at least, the realm where all demons came from. And then he...he....

No control, no hesitation, barely any restraint. Even now, he could recall the warmth of her skin, the specific scent that was only hers washing over him like a tide, the clean, mild taste of her. She'd felt so perfect around him, her taste intoxicating, and the noises she'd made had been fucking *divine*—

The glass shattered in his hand.

Ash stared at the shards that lay on his palm, some embedded in flesh, crimson welling from the wounds. And then he stiffened, shock tensing his spine, but not from the broken pieces.

He was hard again.

*Are you fucking kidding me?*

He shouldn't need to feed again so soon. He shouldn't need to feed at all.

Ash tipped his hand, letting the mess tumble into the garbage before he plucked the remaining shards out of his palm. He left the bloodied pieces in the sink.

There would be time to clean later; he had somewhere more pressing to be.

Ash made a quick detour into the open space that was his bedroom and most of the floor plan. It was spacious and grand, having once functioned as a clock tower before being turned into a penthouse condominium. The design was a strange mismatch between old, abandoned woodwork and modern technology. The kitchen, bathroom, and furniture were all installed by the time he moved in, but the loft above which led into the tower was constructed of the original crossbeams, rickety ironwork stairs, and exposed wood.

He yanked on a pair of dark jeans and a black, long-sleeved shirt; much warmer than the tank and worn sweatpants he'd been wearing before. There hadn't been time to dress. He'd raced up the stairs and leapt off the rooftop as soon as he'd sensed the lurking presence of a demon near the girl.

*Woman.* She was a woman now—a fact Ash should have kept at the front of his goddamn mind before running off. He'd had no plan, no forethought into the aftermath of such a blatant attack by another demon. Getting close to her had been unavoidable. And, in his infinite foolishness, he'd thought he could handle it.

Banishing an *Alpen* didn't require a dress code, but for his next destination, Ash wanted to be wearing actual pants.

He threaded his folded wings through the holes cut out of the back of his shirt. There wasn't time to make himself more humanly presentable and take a cab downtown, not when he had a direct path at night.

The iron-wrought stairs creaked beneath him, and the sting of the autumn breeze tugged at his hair once he returned to the roof.

His wings spread wide, he flapped once, hard enough to send the air rushing away from him, and he leapt.

The leather webbing between the "fingers" of the wings caught air, and he flew over Elliot Bay using a combination of hard flapping and angled gliding. The harbor lights exposed the shape of the water like glowing connect-the-dots before he passed back over the curve of the island to Belltown.

The Space Needle towered close enough that Ash could spot the individual benches inside, empty at this late hour but still lit like a beacon over the water.

Ash liked flying at night—not that he had a choice with how visible he would have been during the day. Plus, the seagulls would be hell to dodge while gliding between skyscrapers. Even now, he had to keep an eye out for the occasional nocturnal gull. They didn't appreciate his presence, especially if he flew unknowingly close to their rooftop nests, and he'd been dive-bombed more than once. Ash couldn't help but be a little fond of the brash, fearless birds, even if their attitude toward him was "kill on sight."

He arrived at his destination near Lenora Street, his boots meeting the roof with heavy impatience. Glass domes that made up the various observatories and greenhouses illuminated his path and guided his way to the rooftop access door.

Unable to enter without permission, he grabbed the golden knocker shaped like an eclipsed sun and banged it against the metal door. His previous fear curdled into simmering anger, and he knew exactly where to aim it.

He waited a minute, two minutes, before footsteps from two floors below drew near, slower than he would have liked. Ash took a step back, shoes scuffing against the stone roof as he settled his weight towards the balls of his feet.

The door opened, and he blinked from the glaring lights beyond. After adjusting to the bright intrusion, he focused on the person in the doorway.

She was a short, sturdy woman, her skin weathered and brown like the bark of a cypress tree. She wore robes the shade of buckskin, simple tan boots, and a sash around her waist that cinched at the front. Her only adornment was the necklace of colorful beads and river shells that hung from her neck. Her dark hair was streaked with gray, giving it a grandmotherly appearance, but any perceived softness ended there. Her hair was tied in a severe knot, her expression stiff as she craned her neck to meet his gaze.

Despite the difference in height, Ash always felt as if she were looking down on him. This was no exception.

"Norbu," he greeted.

"Spiros," the older woman responded, sounding as pleased to see Ash as Ash was to be there. "You're early."

"I'm not here for that. Where's Lazuli?"

She eyed him, brows tight and lips drawn into a frown. Ash didn't blame her suspicion, but he also lacked the time for it.

"He's occupied at the moment. Is there something I can help you with?" She took in his ruffled appearance once more and added, "Are you certain you don't need another dose?"

Ash tried to keep his lips from curling with displeasure, but they did, all the same. "I need to speak to him. *Now.*"

The sharp edge in Norbu's expression on any other day would have made him rethink his words, but this wasn't any other day.

"If you could tell me what this matter is about—"

"The last batch he gave me was bad," Ash cut her off. "It didn't work."

That got her attention. "Come in."

*Finally.*

She stepped back and held the door open for him. He moved through the threshold arch and shortened his stride so he wasn't moving like a stalking, hunting predator. Years of practice didn't shake old habits.

Ash paused and moved aside, pulling in his wings tight against his back as he let Norbu take the lead. The woman gave him a cursory glance but said nothing more as she led him deeper into the building. A building which, on the outside, resembled a typical skyscraper at the edge of Downtown Seattle, with a cramped rooftop access and a pair of metal stairs leading downward.

The stairway, dank and dim now that they'd moved past the unusually bright fluorescent lights at the entrance, continued for two flights until they ended at a landing with another door. Despite the building being at least twenty floors, the stairway did not continue further.

Norbu pulled a ring of keys—ranging from small locker keys to long, elaborate keys made of iron, steel, and in one case, copper—from the thick sash around her waist.

She used an ordinary key on the metal door, opened it for them both, and shut it behind Ash once he stepped through. The space beyond was large, empty, and concrete on all sides. The room would be unremarkable if not for the double doors that didn't belong in any modern commercial building.

The doors stood at nearly ten feet, constructed of rich wood the color of acorns, inlaid with golden etchings that shimmered in the overhead light. Symbols and designs carved their surface, some gilded in gold while others shimmered with something that was felt rather than seen.

There was no key to unlock this door. Norbu laid her hand

on its surface, and the door groaned inward, letting a shaft of bright light filter through. She pushed it open until she could walk through it comfortably and held it open for Ash. She didn't do so out of politeness. If he attempted to walk over that threshold without what the door viewed as Norbu's permission, he would find himself on the receiving end of its wrath.

That was what Ash had been told, and he knew enough about the Tower to avoid pissing off its doors.

Ash walked inside, shivering as some unseen judgement swept over him and deemed him worthy enough to pass. Norbu shut the door behind him, cutting off one world and leading him to another.

The entrance vestibule was large and elegant, constructed of wooden beams and stones. The ceiling above was a long, oval glass dome, glittering with stars between the metalwork panes. Ash knew they were somewhere else, as those stars didn't belong to any constellations he recognized, and they were supposedly two floors away from the rooftop. When he'd asked the Eterna about it the first time he'd gone this way, she'd merely said, "Those are not your stars. And this is not your dream."

As with most things the Eterna used to say, he had no idea what she meant.

The elegance continued as Norbu led them down a spiral staircase constructed of copper banisters and marble steps. Busts sat in alcoves, depicting notable past members, and massive bookshelves lined the circular bottom of the stairwell in what appeared to be an impromptu reading room. Even this far from the bustle of the main areas, the Vates didn't want to be without their books. Ash had found reading nooks tucked away in the strangest of places.

Intricate tapestries complemented the stone walls, with

complex glyphs etched into the arches and baseboards of every massive room. Everything from the banisters to the carpet runners to the golden candelabras gave off a warm, fiery glow that felt majestic rather than aggressive.

They passed through the Artifact Room, Norbu's eyes remaining forward but Ash's attention straying from his path. He'd only seen the room a handful of times, and he wished he had the chance to spend a full day there reading the descriptions of arcane items kept locked away in thick glass trophy cases.

Not for the first time, objects awakened at his presence. A quill made of vulture feathers, a mantlepiece clock constructed of giant baobab wood, a black umbrella that only opened the wrong way; they whirred, clicked, or trembled toward him in a way that felt quite judgmental for objects without faces.

Ash quickened his pace and stayed closer to his guide. The presence of glyphs, both hidden out of sight and visibly carved above the doorways, made the hairs on his neck stiff as his flesh crawled. Ash never truly relaxed until he departed the Tower, and a lingering sense of disappointment stayed with him each time.

Ash wondered if Samara would like it here, and immediately thought, *of course she would.* The girl had a habit of turning curiosity into a chance to shorten her lifespan. Wasn't tonight proof of that?

Norbu led him deeper into the middle of the Tower, well-lit with glowing bauble chandeliers and wall torches that never seemed to need refilling. There was no access to natural daylight in any of the areas he visited, and Ash wondered if that was intentional, a precaution in case Ash decided to throw Lazuli out a window. Smart move.

"Wait here," Norbu instructed when they reached a circular

antechamber with several doors lining the walls and the ceiling high above them. "It won't be long."

*Don't leave this room or cause any trouble,* was what he heard, unspoken but clear as an icy stream.

Closing a pair of heavy dark wood doors behind her, she left him there alone. He made a slow circuit around the room, the tip of his tail twitching. He had to lift his boots so they didn't snag the expensive-looking crimson rug, though he was tempted to put runs in it.

After several long minutes, when Ash grew certain the walls were watching him, footfalls approached from a different pair of doors. He positioned himself without thought—back to the wall, all entrances within line of sight, assessing an exit strategy.

The doors opened, and Lazuli strode into the room. His movements were measured with confidence, his chin held firm but not foolishly high. His sapphire half-cape was trimmed in silver thread, his trousers and robes made of exquisite gold and white fabric, displaying his status within the Order. His brown hair was perfectly coifed, face smooth and absent of stubble, and his eyes were bright and held an expression that Ash could only describe as haughty.

Leader of the Vates of the Eternal Order, ruling over thousands of magic-wielders the world over, and responsible for the first and only line of defense against invasion.

He was barely eighteen years old.

"Ashley," Lazuli greeted him upon entering. "This is a surprise. Must be important for a visit at half past three in the morning."

The Inumerator spoke with unconcerned ease, as if a demon landing on his doorstep was of little consequence. Ash had known kids like that, a few of them his own students, ones that thought what they lacked in experience could be made up for in unearned confidence and bull-headed tenacity.

"This couldn't be done over the phone?" Lazuli added, proving Ash's point.

"The batch you gave me was a dud." What a goddamn understatement. "You have to fix it."

The Inumerator arched an eyebrow, the picture of graceful perplexity.

"Already? Didn't Master Helictite make an adjustment, oh, I'd say...two years ago? I suppose it was only a matter of time until you developed a tolerance. How long ago did it wear off? I could increase the dosage, but it's late, you'll have to wait until—"

The kid was going a mile a minute, his previous aloofness disappearing under his genuine curiosity.

Ash cut through his enthusiasm like a knife. "You don't get it."

He ground his teeth, folded wings rustling against his back as his tail writhed like a trapped serpent. "It stopped working. *Completely.*"

Lazuli blinked and glanced at Norbu, who had stayed for the conversation as his second-in-command. But the other Vate gave a small shrug, and Lazuli turned to Ash with a *smile* of all things. "I'm not sure I take your meaning."

"I'm saying, the batch failed. I'm saying, I had an *epulum.* I'm saying, Lazuli, that I am a threat to everyone around me because the last dose you gave me didn't work. Do you take my goddamn meaning *now?*"

Norbu's eyes were sharp as blades, but Lazuli looked as if Ash had slapped him across the face.

Ash rubbed his forehead with the heel of his palm. *Get a fucking grip.* His tail swayed in agitation, and he forced it still before it could knock over some no-doubt priceless magical vase or whatever.

"I'm sorry," Ash said, the weariness bleeding into his words. "It's been a really, really long night, and I shouldn't have—"

"Spiros." Lazuli's voice was awfully quiet, and far too serious for his young years. "Have you violated the terms of your agreement?"

Ice crept along his veins, a winter storm shrouding his thoughts and freezing his body. Lazuli was asking if Ash had fed. If he'd seduced, ensnared, and drained the energy from a human, breaking the oath he had sworn.

And he had, Ash absolutely had, in the most fucked up way imaginable, with the last person he would have wanted it to happen to.

"No," Ash lied. "Of course not."

Lazuli took a slow breath, and the tension eased from his shoulders. But Norbu continued to appraise Ash with a look that made him want to curl up in his wings and pretend everything was fine.

"If you were in a state of *epulum,* how did you end it?" she asked.

Ash didn't have an answer for that. Demonic frenzies didn't stop by themselves, they had to be sated through a feeding, and the Vates knew that.

Of course, there'd been nothing *typical* about this hunger. They were supposed to be gradual, like a gnawing emptiness or growing thirst, but this one had been the flick of a switch. One minute, he'd been fine. The next, it had been like a dam breaking free, as if twenty-five years of non-feeding had caught up to him, and it was a wonder he hadn't killed Samara in the process.

Norbu still waited. Ash scrambled for a believable lie and snatched the simplest one he could find.

He shrugged. "I'm not sure. It happened only an hour ago. I waited, afraid to leave my place, and it just kind of...settled."

Ash was a passable liar; one didn't spend two decades in the equivalent of witness protection and not learn how to bend the truth. But Norbu's stare didn't ease, and Ash had wielded that disbelieving glare plenty of times on his own students. He should have been immune to its effects, but Norbu was *good.* Much better than Ash had ever been.

"Why didn't you contact us immediately?"

Ash liked Norbu most of the time, but right now, he wished she wasn't so damn competent.

"I didn't think about it."

That was sort of true.

"I panicked."

*Definitely true.*

Norbu opened her mouth, but Lazuli stepped forward, his earlier uncertainty replaced by a don't-worry-I-have-it-all-under-control expression that Ash didn't believe for a second. "Well, you did the right thing by remaining in isolation until it passed. I would hate to think what would have happened if you'd been near anyone at the time."

Ash swallowed. *Yeah. Right.*

"So, can you do anything about it?"

"Of course," the Inumerator said in smooth repose. "I would suggest you stay here until I have it ready. I'll have to tweak the formula a bit, make it more potent. You understand this will increase the side effects, yes?"

Ash hesitated. The side effects, they were...gone. The fog covering the edges of his thoughts, the weakening of his limbs, the lessening of all his senses. He was at full strength again, and he'd felt that way since he'd fed on Samara.

He pressed his lips tight to stop the horrified laugh before it could be born. He nodded wordlessly.

"Excellent." Lazuli supplied a smile and too much enthusiasm. "I'll get right to it."

*You should be celebrating your high school graduation,* Ash thought. *Applying to your favorite pick of colleges. Spending time with your friends and lamenting over a crush that will last until the end of that one remaining golden summer.*

But Ash had to treat Lazuli as the leader he was, not the kid Ash wished he could be. "Thank you, Lazuli. And...I apologize again. Your help is appreciated."

The Inumerator waved a hand at him, unflappable as always. Or at least, that was the image he projected. Ash didn't buy it entirely, but he understood the need to appear unbothered and in control. High school students would eat you alive otherwise.

"Nothing to forgive," Lazuli assured him. "You've had a stressful night. Take a seat, relax. Request some of the chamomile tea if you prefer, and you'll be back home in a couple of hours."

They left Ash then, alone. He didn't mind the solitude, preferred it really, but he could never truly relax in this place. The Vates had been nothing but kind to him, but he had the sense the Tower knew exactly what he was and would always see him as the enemy.

Maybe it had a point. He had fed again, had lied about it, and would continue to lie about it. As long as there were threats out there worse than him, he needed to protect her, and he couldn't do that if the Vates locked him away. Or worse.

He hoped the new dosage would keep him under control, otherwise Ash didn't know what he would do. There was a more permanent solution, of course. It wouldn't even be the first time he'd died.

But if Ash was gone, returned to that hellscape where his kind went after a banishing, who would watch over her? He was a flawed protector, dangerous by his very nature, but to leave Samara exposed and alone would require a coldness he didn't have. Even if it was kinder to her in the end.

When Lazuli returned carrying a dark red, velvet pouch, Ash accepted it and kept his silence.

## CHAPTER FIVE

# ASH

PRESENT

"What the hell is *this?*"

Ash waited for her to answer, scrutinized her from his place on the couch. He didn't trust himself to move closer. Even from across the living room, he caught her unmistakable scent, her own specific flavor. To Ash, it smelled like the heavy air before rain.

It was a scent he didn't think he'd sample so close again, but here he was, probably about to make another mistake. But there'd been this persistent tug at the back of his mind, the need to check on Samara, to make sure that night hadn't caused any lasting harm.

Ash certainly hadn't expected to crawl through her apartment window to find his own face plastered all over the papers on her coffee table. The Eterna had shown him the articles a long time ago, but it was still a shock to see them in *her* possession.

She snapped out of her wide-eyed stare when the container of food—doughnuts, by the smell of it—slipped from her hands and hit the linoleum. Wincing, she leaned down and scooped up the box, placing it on the counter before staring at him again. She wasn't screaming, so that was something.

He gripped the edge of her sofa, the tips of his nails digging into the fabric, attempting to ground himself and not vault across the room at her. Ash's mouth flooded with saliva, and he had to force himself still.

*Fuck.* This was a mistake. He shouldn't have come.

"What?" Her voice was faint, as if she'd been distracted by something else and only now noticed him.

His annoyance flared.

"What is this?" Ash motioned at the papers scattered on the table. "What did you do?"

"What does it look like?" Her gaze hardened, her voice setting to match. "You didn't exactly leave me a choice."

"You...remember me?"

"Yeah, I do. Sorta. What the *hell* did you do to me?"

A hard lump lodged in his throat, and a part of himself gleefully chimed, *She remembers. You're not going to get away with it.*

Instead, he pretended her question hadn't nearly shattered the ground beneath him and asked, "What do you recall from that night?"

She breathed hard, her chest rising and falling like she was in the midst of combat with an enemy on the battlefield.

It was tantalizingly familiar, hearing her panted breath. Ash gripped the couch tighter.

But she didn't run out the door, and when she realized her home invader wasn't going to attack her, she gathered her composure with impressive speed.

"My memories, they...they don't make sense. I thought I was going crazy." Samara paused, and when he didn't respond, her composure started to crumble, leaving the rest of her words unsteady. "Or that you were some kind of sick asshole who had drugged me and...and..."

"And what?" he asked, even as dread coiled in his gut. That was familiar, too. "Took advantage of you?"

Her face twisted into something painful, and surprisingly, pleading. "Did you?"

Her voice cracked, but she didn't cry. Didn't break down into sobs when so many others would have.

Ash was slow to respond, his voice halting. "That...is a complicated question."

"It seems pretty goddamn straightforward to me."

There was the fire he was familiar with. He was glad to see it hadn't burned out of her completely, even if it was aimed at him.

"By the definition of the word, yes."

Her face fell, and he added, as if an aside, "But I didn't want to."

"You didn't want to?"

"No."

"Did you do it because you're a demon?"

He almost smiled, but the gesture quickly died. "Yes."

Samara's memories might be obscured, but Ash remembered everything from that night. Trapping her against the mattress, sinking into her until there was no space between them, devouring her until she begged and cried for more—

No, *no.* This was not how it was supposed to go. He'd been fine until she'd walked in. Agitated, guilty, but not riddled with need as he was now, the ache surging through him as soon as she'd walked through the door.

She wanted answers? Ash was just as lost.

"You didn't want to do it," she repeated, and he could almost see the wheels turning in her head, taking the information given and dissecting it. "You didn't want to hurt me."

He winced, but she wasn't looking at him, her musings turned inward. Samara was trying to solve a problem she didn't understand and couldn't possibly fix. Ash himself didn't know how to fix it, though God knows he'd tried.

The Vates's formula should have worked. It had always worked, and Ash thought it had for a while. The two weeks after his relapse had been business as usual, and he'd hoped Halloween night had been a fluke. By the third week, the hunger had grown, little by little, until the last few days left him pacing around the clock tower, half-mad with fantasies that wouldn't leave his head.

Even now, they curled around his thoughts, tantalizing and vivid. He saw himself grabbing her by the shoulders and pushing her down onto the nearest surface, ripping off only enough clothing to take what he needed.

*Goddamnit, you're doing it again.*

There was a growing realization inside him, and dread sprouted alongside it. Had he truly come here to make sure she was fine? Or was that the lie he told himself to get her alone a second time?

"It doesn't matter," Ash growled, because it truly didn't. His good intentions were nothing in the face of his hunger, as he was discovering much too late. "You should have left it alone."

He rose to his feet, hands balled into fists so he wouldn't be tempted to reach for her, touch her, caress his fingers over her warm skin to claim what should be his—

*Stop it.*

He needed to leave. Why was he still here?

"There's nothing in those files that can help you," he

managed through clenched teeth, "and you'll only attract the wrong kind of attention."

Samara tilted her head, her nose scrunched. "Do you not count two demons in my bedroom as the wrong kind of attention?"

Against all good sense and rational thought, she took a step towards him. Ash immediately retreated, even as his body howled at him to do the opposite, and the back of his heel bumped the couch. He had nowhere to go, and his tail lashed out like a cornered animal.

"You need to stop." It was meant to be a warning, but his words came out more panicked than threatening. "Just take a deep breath and calm down."

He knew it was the wrong thing to say before the words fully left his mouth.

"Calm down? You want me to *calm down?* Are you...are you *serious?*" Her hands curled into fists at her sides, and to his alarm, her eyes were glassy with unshed tears.

"Look..." He rubbed the back of his neck, wings shifting in a rustle from her standing so close, *too* close. "What happened that night was my fault. Something went wrong when I tried to erase your memory of the *Alp* and me. I'm trying to get a handle on it, but I'm not screwing around when I say you need to relax. The more frustrated you are, the worse it gets."

"The worse *what* gets?" she demanded, throwing out her arms for emphasis. "You haven't even told me what happened!"

Ash closed his eyes and attempted to summon the strength to remain focused and calm, since she was unable to do so. He should have been more understanding. Of course she was confused, even more than he was, and he needed to have patience. He used to be *good* at this sort of thing.

Unfortunately, now was not the time to explain the nuances of his demonic nature. Ash's self-control slipped with each moment, as if it were a tangible thing he felt sliding out of his grasp. He had seen for himself that Samara was fine—even if she was remembering glimpses of that night, which shouldn't be possible. And now that he knew, he had a whole new set of complications to stress about.

Ash's hunger was fast approaching, but it wasn't there yet. He still had time to get the hell out.

He opened his eyes and looked past her into the dark hallway, but there was no sign of the hobgoblin. Ash could smell it had been in the apartment recently, and he wished the damn thing would come out and soothe its master. Weren't they supposed to guard their owners from demons?

Even if it had tolerated Ash after he'd banished the *Alp*, it should have perceived him as a threat after he'd fed on Samara.

But no, the stupid beast was gone, and now Ash had to calm her without touching her or getting anywhere near her. He was tempted to slip out her bedroom window again, or hell, go for the living room balcony; it was much closer.

Against his will, Ash's gaze found her face again. It had been a long time since someone had read him the riot act. The Vates did little more than watch him as if he might steal the silverware or possibly eat a child, and here she was, looking like she was winding up to deck him across the jaw.

It should not have been so arousing, but here *he* was, tail curling with interest as his tongue swiped over his sharp teeth.

"You're not going to tell me, are you?" Her face pinched into a grimace. "I'm already involved in this, whatever *this* is, and you're going to keep me in the dark. Are you going to try to wipe my memory again?"

"What? No, obviously not—"

"Then why are you here?" The words were low, but her frustration spoke at a loud volume. "Why did you come back after what you did? After what you're *still* doing to me?"

He frowned, his confusion great enough to temporarily sidetrack his hunger. "What are you talking about?"

"You *know.*" She crossed her arms over her stomach as if to steel herself against some imperceptible chill. "I went to the doctor. They gave me antibiotics and said to go to the ER. But that won't help, will it?"

The way she stood, her arms folded in close, hiding her hands under her arms. Dread crawled up Ash's spine.

"I don't understand," he tried, steady as if not to startle a spooked horse. "If you tell me, explain it to me, then maybe I can...figure something out."

*Maybe I can help you,* Ash didn't say. Even if he could be near her without wanting to get between her legs, which was a pretty big fucking *if* right now, she wouldn't want anything to do with him.

As if to prove his point, she shook her head and took a step back, placing distance between them.

"You did this to me," Samara said, a small tremble in her voice. "You did. Why are you acting like you don't have any idea what I'm saying?"

She braced a hand against her forehead, and her words carried a slow, muddled quality to them. "Why me? Why did this happen to me? Was it the thing I did as a kid? The Ouija board bullshit? Is that it? Why did you...What did you *do* to me?"

Ash sensed it again, the overwhelming sensation of something terribly wrong. Instinct spurred him forward, urged him to close the last few feet between them and take what was his.

*No.* She wasn't *his.* She was his charge, yes, his responsibility. He had debts he owed, and he was supposed to pay them, not accrue more. He couldn't—

But she was *right there.* All he had to do was...

Ash realized too late he was standing over her, his body acting on its own, wings half-spread in a position that was entirely possessive. His tail undulated back and forth, the incubus part of him impatient for another taste. Once hadn't been enough.

Samara didn't move, frozen and staring upward with wide eyes, lips parted. Her taste was already on his tongue.

"Let me see it." This time his words were a command.

She shuddered, as if physically compelled to obey, but she hugged her arms tighter across her middle. And then she screamed. Hunched over as if stabbed in the gut, she wailed, sharp and pitched in unrelenting agony.

Ash clapped a hand over her mouth and spun her around so she was pinned to his chest, his other arm around her waist in support as her knees buckled a second later.

Burning flesh assailed his nose and smoke curled from the edge of the glove around her clenched right fist. Ash forced open her fingers and yanked off the glove, finding her hand bandaged beneath. He peeled off the tape stuck to her skin, trying his best not to hurt her, but she still screamed as he pulled off the bandage and exposed the thing that called to him in unholy harmony.

It glowed like hot coals embedded in her skin, staring back at him in a mockery of his own mark, carved into her flesh just as it had been carved into his.

A demonic *signum*.

The shock of it was like being doused with ice water, and for a moment, Ash was thrown back into his right mind. The air rushed out of him, and all he could think was, *No, no, no, no. It's not real. It can't be.*

But not only was it there, it was activated, visiting upon her the punishment for disobeying one's master.

Ash knew exactly what that felt like.

Who had found her? Everyone who had a hand in his transformation, or once had access to his old mission deployments, was either dead or had disappeared. But someone must have reopened the project and continued the work. He had to get her to Lazuli. Broken oaths and unfulfilled bargains didn't matter, not now.

Ash's tumultuous thoughts ground to a halt. Samara was no longer screaming. She was completely motionless.

And then she wasn't. She arched her back, pushing against him as if remaining still was agony. Her breath hitched, uneven, and her arousal hit his senses like a wave breaking for shore.

Ash spun her around and gripped her by the arms, glaring down at her, nostrils flaring as he took in the sight. She was disheveled, and sweating, and never more appealing than in that moment. The rhythmic pulse in her neck, the glistening of her skin, and the hazy heat in her eyes acted like a siren's song. He wouldn't be satisfied until he dragged his teeth over her and tasted every inch.

The grimace of pain was gone from her expression. The *signum* must have finished doling out its punishment for now, but the symbol still smoldered on her skin, shimmering as if fire made its home just under the surface.

Samara wavered on her feet, and she only remained standing because of his vise-like hold. Her cheeks were flushed, her words a strained, desperate plea. It pulled at him with a magnetic force, the delicious nectar of her need reeling him in.

"Don't...leave me like this," she begged. "I don't know what you did to me, but it *hurts.*"

The fragile cracks in her words shattered the last of his resolve, and whatever remained of his control washed away.

Ash hooked his arms under her shoulders and knees and lifted her off the ground. Even against his significant heat, she burned, her heady aroma rising in intoxicating waves.

*Feed.*

He didn't know if his own body compelled him, or if he was caught in her gravity well, falling faster and faster until he broke upon her surface.

*Give in. Take. Feed.*

Under the sway of the mantra of his hunger, Ash carried her into the bedroom.

# CHAPTER SIX

# ASH

Samara curled against his chest, her eyes shut, fisting his shirt as she buried her face in the sleeve. When Ash set her on the bed, she arched her back and made small, desperate noises at the loss of contact.

The sound drove him mad, and his sharp nails left their marks on his own clothing as he removed them hastily. The part of him that still clung to sanity cried out not to do this, to stop before it was too late. That voice railed against an invisible wall, barred entrance and ignored even as Ash knew he should listen. The last feeding had been an accident; unprepared, he'd been helpless to stop it.

But this was a solid line he dared not cross, because if he did, he was truly damned.

Even with that knowledge, Ash couldn't turn away. The opportunity to run with his tail between his legs had passed. The *epulum* had him in its clutches, and he was as helpless now as he'd been decades ago, trapped and enslaved to a biology he couldn't understand. Ash couldn't stop, couldn't pull away, and even if he could...did he truly want to?

The demonic instinct knew what he needed, even as the human part of him begged for it to stop. Urgency fueled his movements as he quickly undressed her, careful not to leave marks in his haste this time. He tugged off her shoes, her pants, her bra and blouse.

All the while, her hands were on his chest, pushing him away or searching for something to brace against. Samara whimpered, "Make it stop," over and over. She seemed to be in the thralls of the *epulum* herself, writhing on the bed as if burning from the inside out.

What remained of his humanity, however distant that may be, wanted to take her in his arms and hold her tight, tell her things that would soothe her fear. But that wasn't the part of Ash that had control, and the demon had no patience for sweet words and soft caresses.

Ash stopped himself long enough to see her, not the nakedness of her body but what she held in her eyes. She looked to him for answers, for something to hold onto, a child needing reassurance that there were no monsters waiting for her in the dark.

But she'd learned long ago that monsters were real, and they didn't always remain in shadow. It was a lesson she'd forgotten because of him, so perhaps he was to blame after all.

Ash leaned down, like a lion hovering over a fallen gazelle. And he kissed her.

Her lips were soft and parted in surprise, and she surprised *him* by surging up to meet him, pressing forcefully against his mouth with a hunger of her own. The predator in him purred as he licked her mouth, savoring her taste, but it wasn't enough.

He shouldn't have kissed her, but what did it matter? Even if she again resisted the amnestic effects of an incubus feeding, a stolen kiss was the least of the sins he was about to commit.

When he separated from her lips, she frowned, and it would have been sweet in another situation, another lifetime. At least the tears caused by her pain were gone, and that was all he could manage; Ash couldn't wait a minute longer.

His cock was painfully hard and dribbling pre-cum, which he spread over his shaft, the clear liquid thick and viscous. The self-lubrication part of his anatomy would make this easier for her, physically if not mentally.

Kneeling between her legs, Ash switched hands, bringing his slick fingers to her labia and pressing between them. The groan she made forced him to grit his teeth and squeeze the base of his shaft. He wouldn't be able to come until she did, but he hoped the pressure would ease the agonizing sensation.

He slipped his fingers inside her with the intent of lubrication but found it unnecessary. She was wetter than he expected—but did he even know what to expect? None of this was *normal.* He should be helping her, not prying her open and feasting, breaking every promise he'd made to her, whether she was aware of those promises or not.

Ash bit down on his lip, fighting with every last shred of his control, but it wasn't enough. It never was.

Pushing the tip of his cock against her entrance, and without a word of warning or comfort, he pushed inside. He didn't pause, even when Samara gripped the sheets and released a sob. He didn't know if it was from pain or pleasure, but it broke him either way.

As soon as he was embedded deep within her, his humanity receded. The demonic side of him reveled as she lifted her hips so he could slide into her that much easier.

Such willing, eager prey.

He bottomed out, his vision narrowing into dark tunnels. His hips pressed hard against hers. She was wound so tight around him he could hardly breathe, and it was an unholy pleasure that was worthy of a lightning bolt from God's own hand.

Samara gasped, small tremors moving through her muscles. Ash pulled her hips higher, obeying an instinct that whispered insidiously in his mind, and he gripped his left hand in her right, threading their fingers together. He sensed her *signum* on the other side, catalyzed with heat, and his own *signum* throbbed in answer.

Her body relaxed under his, and she released a soft sigh, as if she felt it too. Ash ran his tongue along the soft skin between her neck and shoulder, wholly unnecessary to the feeding, but he couldn't stop touching her, tasting her.

Samara craned her neck as if to give him room, as if she wanted him there, and his careful tenderness vanished along with the demon's control.

Ash squeezed her hips in his claws, hoisted both her legs over his shoulders, and thrust hard.

Samara cried, her body tense again but unable to move, completely pinned as he fucked her as he pleased. Electric flashes echoed up his spine. His wings half-flared as if he was about to take flight.

Devouring, carnal, rhythmic—like two mindless beasts who cared for nothing but the rutting bliss of their union. It was building in her just as it was building in him, a tandem climb where she led and he followed, pulled by an unbreakable thread. Each tug of the cord dragged him into existential bliss, and it wouldn't compare to what lay at the precipice.

With one hand trapped in his, she used the other to grip his arm, her mouth open, gulping air as her eyes squeezed tight.

Ash knew she was close, not just from her taut muscles but from the energy building inside her. It was the electricity gathering in the air under a massive thunderhead, about to burst with violent destruction.

He needed that downpour, or his pleasure would build and build with nowhere to go. Torture and ecstasy, he didn't want it to stop. The sex was grounding, it was alive. It was human.

What came next wasn't.

With his free hand, Ash yanked her hair and wrenched her head back, exposing her neck.

*"Meus es tu,"* he growled against the column of her throat, letting his sharp teeth graze her skin. *"Meus es tu."*

It was declaration more than command, but by the visceral reaction of her body, she took it as one.

The dam burst, and Ash was nearly swept away in a tide of molten current. It poured into him, a salvation prayed for, like a dying man envisioning an oasis before stumbling upon it.

Samara gripped the sheets like a lifeline, her cries jagged as she braced against the bed, spine arched, and she squeezed around him so tightly he couldn't move—

No, he couldn't move because the knot at the base of his shaft swelled, trapping him up to the hilt. Panic was a distant concept; all he could do was groan against her neck, the energy still pouring into him like flood gates shattered. It was a deluge in which he would gladly drown.

Ash opened his eyes wide and, oh, *there* was the panic. It was too much, he was draining her, and he couldn't stop, not when he was fucking *stuck.* He'd managed to avoid trapping her the first time, probably because it had happened so fast and caught him by surprise. That night had also lacked the peculiar intensity of this feeding.

She was just as caught, throbbing around him as he continued to pull energy from deep within her. Samara's writhing weakened, dejected noises in her throat as the pleasure continued to tug at her.

It tugged at him too, and before he could stop himself, he bit down on the junction of her shoulder and neck. Christ knows why he did it, but the sinful noise she made forced another spurt of come from him, and he crossed over from sensitive to sore.

Finally, after a stretch of moments that could have continued for a lifetime, the energy tapered and his body came down from its cyclic, pulsing high. His skin tingled, his muscles heavy with soothing, liquid warmth, and his tail hung limp across the bedspread.

An addictive sensation, but more than pleasure. It was healing. No more muscle soreness or headaches from the Vates's concoction—the side effects which persisted while the suppression of hormones had continued to fail.

The knot deflated enough for Ash to pull out, copious amounts of semen spilling free. The demon part of him, sated and fuller than it had ever been before, curled up like a cat and went to sleep.

Lucidity returned to him, and all the horror that came with it.

"S...Samara?"

There wasn't so much as a flicker behind her eyelids, her body limp and pliant under him.

*Shit. Shit, shit, shit!*

Ash hunched over her, took a breath, and listened. Her breathing was slow but deep, and her heartbeat, more felt than heard, was steady and strong.

Ash released the breath, and his own heart started up again as he sat back on his heels. She was unconscious, but alive.

The shame returned, bitter and sickening on his tongue, and he assessed the rest of the damage done to her.

He thought he'd been careful, but just like the first feeding, he'd left signs of her mishandling. Scratches littered her skin, thin lines of pink and red. The bite mark on her neck wasn't deep, but it had broken skin and would bruise. God only knew what other bruises were going to show up on her tomorrow.

And she might not remember how she'd gotten them. He didn't know for sure—she seemed to remember *something* of their first encounter—but for her sake, he hoped she wouldn't recall a thing about this one. That's how it was supposed to work. The incubi left their victims without any memory of the feeding. That way, they escaped human notice as they moved through the population, feasting without starting a panic.

But there were legends and stories about incubi, succubi and other demons that fed from sex, so clearly, the amnestic effect sometimes failed. Or perhaps, some people were more resistant to demonic influence. He certainly didn't know, and asking the Vates would be tantamount to confessing.

Ash placed the inside of his wrist against her forehead and found she was cooler than the feverish degree she'd been before, her skin no longer flushed or soaked in sweat.

Physically, she might have improved, but that wasn't his only worry. Ash carefully took her hand and studied the *signum*, delicately running his thumb over the design. The previously inflamed lines were now pink and new, as if freshly healed. He didn't know what it meant, but he knew any relief on his part was premature.

Ash lingered, holding this intimate, stolen moment close, like a precious thing. The worried creases around her eyes were smooth in sleep, and the frown that seemed to be a permanent fixture was missing. She looked peaceful, unburdened by the nightmare that circled her like a shark scenting blood.

Something twisted inside him.

*I thought I could protect you from this.*

Ash pulled on his clothing, irritated by the rips in his shirt. At least his jacket had gone unscathed, as he'd left it on her couch. Her clothes were in worse shape due to his lack of patience, and he winced, wondering if he should buy her replacements.

Probably not. How could he explain the state of her clothes if she didn't remember this? And if she did know the truth, new clothing would be poor recompense.

Halloween night, he'd left her naked and asleep, creeping out of her window like a literal thief in the night. He didn't want to leave her like this, but he couldn't bear to touch her again. He'd already destroyed the boundaries of her comfort and safety; he wasn't going to manhandle her in her sleep.

And the longer he lingered, the heavier his heart weighed.

Planning to grab the blanket he'd spotted earlier on the couch, Ash went out to the living room and came to a stop. A gray lump sat on the stack of strewn papers that depicted Ash's human life. Green eyes stared up at him, narrowed in mockery, or maybe smugness.

"Oh," Ash said. "It's you."

The hobgoblin did a slow blink. *Definitely smugness.*

"Don't play stupid. You understand English just fine."

The beast gave no indication either way. Ash went for the blanket and eyed the imposter-cat, but it didn't so much as hiss at him.

"You're not very good at your job, you know that? You should be chasing me out. Leave a scratch or two as a point of pride."

The hobgoblin closed its eyes, and, oh yes, it was smirking.

He left the creature and returned to the bedroom. Samara was still unconscious, her head turned to the side with her hair laying across her neck. He'd always liked the color, almost muted until it caught the sunlight, and then it shone like hidden spun gold. He'd overheard her talking about it once, how she hated the hue, calling it dull dishwater. He couldn't disagree more.

Ash carefully lifted her up to slide the soiled sheets out from under her. He briefly considered burning them, but property destruction wasn't something he needed to add to his list of sins, so he bunched them up and tossed them into the washing machine tucked into a hallway recess.

He pulled the blanket up to her shoulders, wishing he had more for her than paltry gestures. His breath froze as she rolled onto her side and curled into a protective position, but she didn't awaken. She likely wouldn't for several hours.

Against his better judgement, Ash reached down and carefully brushed the hair out of her face. It was all he could offer her: meaningless gestures. His bitterness contrasted with her soft skin against the back of his fingers, her scent clean, no longer tinged with the stench of burning flesh or the sharp tang of intense arousal.

It was just her. And when she woke up, he would no longer exist in her mind.

Ash dropped his hand and pulled away. He spared a glance at the window and its crumpled lock, as well as the pile of blackout curtains in one corner that Samara had apparently abandoned. He'd have to do something about that. Ash had been enough of an asshole; he didn't need to leave her with a broken lock on top of everything else.

He grabbed his jacket off the couch, scooped up the papers after shooing away the hobgoblin, and left Samara's apartment. He locked the door with a skeleton key that looked like it was made of finger bones. It probably was, knowing the Vates. They did love their word play.

What they didn't love was a predatory demon on the loose, yet another problem for Ash to juggle. Going by the state of Samara's mark after the feeding, Ash had bought himself a bit of time. If he could figure out how she had a demonic *signum* and why his destructive appetite had returned, then maybe he could bypass the Vates altogether.

He didn't think Lazuli would punish Samara for what he'd done, but...he couldn't take that chance.

Ash was on his own.

## CHAPTER SEVEN

# SAM

Sunlight filtered through the bedroom, courtesy of Sam having given up on her blackout curtains. She groaned and stretched her arms above her head, curling her toes as her back creaked and her joints popped. There was a lump against her leg—Monster flopped on his side, softly snoring without a care in the world.

Plucking at the blue fleece blanket covering her legs, Sam frowned.

Why was she naked? Where were her clothes? Had she had too much to drink again? It had been a while since she'd achieved that level of drunk. In fact, she hadn't had any alcohol since—

She ripped the blanket off her body. Scratches marked her hips and arms, and her sides were discolored with finger-shaped bruises. Her sheets had been stripped, and she'd have to locate them too.

It was exactly how she'd woken up the morning after Halloween—except this time, she remembered everything. The searing pain in her hand, brutal and punishing, and the cold fear that came with it.

But nothing loomed larger in her mind than Spiros. She'd gotten so much wrong. He hadn't been some stranger from a party or an invader in her home. He wasn't even human.

And yet, that didn't stop what came after.

It had been sex, and also nothing like sex. Every touch had been a spark ignited, her body caught in a blaze that begged for relief, wholly unrecognizable. Sex wasn't something she sought out, and after enough time, she'd forgotten what it was like. Its proclaimed importance was lost on her. To her, the deed rang hollow.

This hadn't been *that.*

Despite the ache in her bones and the soreness of her muscles, there was one source of pain conspicuously absent. Sam stared at the back of her hand, the warmth of Ash's fingers so tangible her mind she kept expecting to see his hand threading hers. Faded to a pink pigmentation, the marked skin was smooth and whole once more. As one finger traced the pattern, she recalled Ash gripping her hand, pushing it into the sheets, and with it bringing instant relief.

It wasn't the only thing that had brought relief, and it couldn't compare to the unnatural bliss of Spiros pushing inside her. It had been like sucking in a lungful of air after suffocation, or a wound drained of burning venom.

She wasn't waxing poetic; whatever he'd done had stopped the fever and cleared her head. Sam rubbed her forehead in an attempt to quell the pressure there. At least she had a decent guess as to what had happened Halloween night, and as confusing as it was, at least one thing was certain.

Spiros hadn't forced himself on her.

Monster twitched and gave a sleepy complaint, and Sam rubbed the soft fur of his belly before getting out of bed. She glanced at the washing machine as she passed, and sure enough, the soiled sheets were inside.

That was...decent of him. An explanation would have been better.

After checking the rest of the apartment to make sure Spiros was truly gone, she hopped into the shower. The scratches stung in the warm water, and she cleaned each one she found. At least she could stop the antibiotic treatment now, or...should she? She didn't know what kind of bacterial cross-contamination could happen with a demon, especially one she'd had sex with. *Twice.*

She winced as she bent her neck forward to rinse her hair. Each twinge of soreness was a reminder of how hard he'd gripped her, stretched her full to the point of exquisite pain. The pressure of his nails digging into her thighs, the sharp pleasure of teeth on her shoulder—it was all there at the forefront of her mind, so clear and sharp, where Halloween night was like an obscure dream.

But it wasn't the graphic images that Sam lingered on, the water streaming down her skin background noise compared to the memory of last night. It was the kiss.

His lips had been soft, gentle, before pressing deeper, his tongue prodding into her mouth. It felt unnecessary. Personal. The sex she could understand, to a point, but why had he kissed her?

It was that memory above all others that forced Sam to turn the knob to biting cold water. The shower helped only so much, but at least she was clean.

After starting the washing machine—her water heater was too cheap to handle a warm shower and wash at the same time—she made herself a bowl of oatmeal and a glass of soy milk. Everything felt almost routine, even down to feeding the cat (was he a cat?) and sitting on the couch to look out the window.

The Seattle skyline was gray and cold, but even in the dreary weather she spotted boats and ferries out in the marina, tiny toy figures at this distance. The sight of the water was soothing no matter what was going on in Sam's life. She absentmindedly pet Monster while she pondered the pile of papers conspicuously absent from her floor. If Spiros thought those were her only copies, then he hadn't evolved past his time in the 1970s.

A phone chime cut through the silence, punctual as ever. It was noon.

*"Hi, sweetie."* The chipper voice on the line was discordant with the gloominess outside. *"How's your Thanksgiving? Enjoying a good book?"*

*Now there's an idea,* Sam thought. Maybe she could find something at the library; there were plenty of cultures that believed in demons, and there might be something insightful she could glean. She could imagine how pleased a certain demon would be, considering how well he'd reacted last night to her self-appointed research project.

He reacted so well he'd ended up in her bed.

Sam shoved the last spoonful of oatmeal into her mouth before swallowing it down.

"Not yet," she said. "But I plan to do lots of reading."

Just not the kind of reading her mom expected of her.

They spoke for a time, Sam focusing on the mundane parts of her life. Work (same as always), TV shows (none since she'd been distracted), how she was doing financially (badly, since forever). Her mother didn't ask if she'd met anyone yet, for which Sam was grateful. Her mom rarely focused on that part of her life, and Sam wasn't sure if she was respecting her privacy, or if she'd given up on the idea of grandchildren.

As they were entering more dangerous territory—the family gathering for Christmas, which would now include Uncle Walter's new mini poodle (making this his fifth), as well as her sister's new baby (who was due any day now)—there was a knock at her door.

Sam frowned. "One second, Mom."

She put the phone on the counter and prepared herself for a battle. It would be Mr. Morris again, complaining about the noise Sam rarely made. Though to be fair, the last noise complaint she'd received had been on Halloween night, and that complaint might have been warranted.

Turning the lock, Sam braced for the wrath of an old bastard and swung open the door.

Spiros stood on her doorstep.

For a moment, Sam thought maybe she was crazy. Had she imagined he was a demon? There was no hint of horn or tail or wing, though that annoyed expression was familiar.

He shifted his weight lightly from one foot to the other, as if trying to find his balance without a tail to aid him.

"What are you doing here?" she blurted. "You look..."

A divot formed between his eyebrows. "You still remember me?"

Sam's frown rivaled his, in degree if not confusion.

"Yes? I very much remember you. *And* last night."

Sam didn't think demons were capable of losing all the color to their faces, but this one did as he glanced quickly up and down the hallway.

"We shouldn't discuss this out here. May I come in?"

She crossed her arms over her chest. Her gaze narrowed

further. “What if I say no?”

“Then I won’t.”

Sam let out a huff, but Spiros didn’t make a move to leave, and she eyed the objects in his arms. A black box of tools in one hand, and a long, thin box tucked under his other arm.

“What’s that?”

“A toolbox.”

She squinted at him. “Why do you have a toolbox?”

He took a deep breath. “Thought I would, you know, fix the lock on your window.”

“My window?”

“I broke it. Getting inside. To stop the *Alp.* Which you probably don’t remember—”

“I do.” She paused. “Mostly. But I didn’t realize my window was broken.”

“Then it’s a good thing I’m here.”

Well, *that* made her want to slam the door in his face, but with the rare November sunshine streaming through the living room window and his human appearance, she felt almost brave. Maybe he really would fix her window and then leave without causing any more problems in Sam’s life.

Plus, between her landlord and a demon, the demon was the more reliable option.

Sam stepped back and held open the door. Spiros raised his brows.

“Do you need an invitation first?” she asked when he didn’t move.

He rolled his eyes. “That’s vampires.”

She assumed he was joking. She didn’t ask.

He passed over the threshold, and Sam couldn’t shake the feeling that a large predator had stepped into the room. She should probably be more alarmed by that, but she wasn't in a financial position to turn down free repairs.

Sam shut the door and followed him, her gaze drawn to his back where his wings should be. No trace of them lay hidden underneath the black windbreaker. Spiros glanced over his shoulder, and she looked away. Her attention landed on the phone still lying on her countertop, lit up from the active call.

*Shit.*

Sam snatched the phone and held it up to her ear.

"Mom? You still there?"

*"I'm here."* Her voice was lilted with interest. *"Who's that?"*

"Uh." Sam turned to the demon. He watched her, expression blank. "No one."

*"Was that a man I heard?"*

*"No,"* Sam emphasized. Definitely *not* a man.

*"You don't need to be embarrassed."*

Sam rubbed her forehead. She had no idea.

"It's just the maintenance guy."

Spiros raised his brows at her flimsy lie.

*"On Thanksgiving?"*

"Yeah. Emergency repair."

*"Oh, no, is everything all right?"*

"Yeah, yeah, it's fine. The lock on my window broke...for some reason." Sam narrowed her eyes. "Gotta fix it so no one crawls in my bedroom at night."

His expression tightened, and then his face smoothed into unreadable blankness so quickly Sam wondered how much practice he had doing that.

*"All right, dear, I'll let you go. Don't want to distract you while the repairman is there."*

"You're fine." Sam turned away so she'd have the illusion of privacy. "It's just something I need to take care of. I'll talk to you later, Mom. Love you. Happy Thanksgiving."

*"Love you too, sweetie. Enjoy your holiday and let me know how the repairs go."*

After hanging up, Sam took her time to place her phone in her pocket. The awkwardness of the situation was not something she was prepared for, but perhaps she could take comfort in the fact he didn't seem too thrilled either.

Sam turned and opened her mouth to speak, something along the lines of *can we make this quick?*

She shut her mouth. Spiros had vanished, and the sound of splintering wood signaled where he'd gone.

*Okay,* she thought, and followed the noise of destruction to her bedroom.

CHAPTER EIGHT

# SAM

Spiros was pulling the ruined lock from the windowsill when Sam entered the bedroom, but that wasn't what drew her full stare.

Thick, leathery wings folded against his back, the tips of them nearly brushing the floor. His tail flicked across her carpet, the movements quick and irritated as if it didn't enjoy the texture. His pointed fingernails traced over the damaged frame of the window as carefully as if they were surgeon's tools.

He was...striking. He was also less terrifying in the light of day. His jacket hung off the back of her desk chair, exposing the noticeable lines of his toned arms and shoulders. The curves of his swept-back horns were nearly illuminated in the sunlight, and they reminded Sam of a regal, half-formed crown made of stone. That, or a cat's ears turned back in irritation. It was hard to decide which.

The buttery light through the open window filtered through his wings, and instead of the solid, leathery mass she expected, she saw thin bones and blood vessels, delicately shaped like the veins of a dried leaf.

The creases of his face were no longer severe when they weren't draped in shadow. It was a handsome face, even with the permanent, vague scowl. His wings and tail, which she'd thought of as monochrome gray, were more of a slate or granite color, with specks of silver flecked along their surface.

Yes, that's what he reminded her of. Not fire and brimstone and evil incarnate, but something formed from stone, sturdy and natural. His scent was faint, but always present. Earthy soil, dark wood, and fresh air—like being on a mountainside—isolated, far from humanity, cold, but also beautiful.

Perhaps all demons were like this. Then again, she'd only met two, and one of them had teeth for a face.

He didn't look at her, but his tone was clipped. "Shouldn't take more than an hour, then I'll be out of your hair."

"Uh. That's fine. You don't need to rush."

He shrugged and said, "Figured you'd want to be out for the holiday."

The bitter words tumbled out like poison on her tongue. "I thought you've been following me since I was a kid. Wouldn't you know I don't have anywhere else to be?"

The silence hung between them like a smothering weight. Somehow, Sam had made a conversation with a demon even more uncomfortable.

Except he didn't look uncomfortable. He seemed more annoyed than anything, and she got the impression of a teacher waiting for an unruly student to be done with a tantrum.

She sat on the bed if only to do something other than look at his face, but the silence grew too long for Sam's liking, and she twisted her hands in her lap.

"You've really been keeping an eye on me this whole time?"

His answer was more question than statement. "Yes?"

Well, it was as good an opening as any.

"If I...freed you, or whatever, twenty-five years ago, where have you been until now? Hopefully not sitting outside my window."

His eyes narrowed, but there was a suspicious twitch at the corner of his mouth. "No. I do have a life outside of making sure you're still breathing."

"Looking like that?"

He rolled his eyes. "Obviously not. Watch."

Spiros tightened his jaw and closed his eyes. The wings were the most obvious; they folded inwards and then disappeared behind him accompanied by an uncomfortable noise of bones and muscles moving in ways they shouldn't. The horns retreated into his temples, and his tail vanished from view. His nails smoothed, and even his ears rounded into soft human ones.

Sam got to her feet and approached him, a hand outstretched to touch...what, she didn't know.

He flinched. She let her hand fall to her side.

"Sorry," she said, not sure what she was apologizing for. Maybe it was the feral-dog look on his face, deciding if an extended hand warranted a lick or a bite.

He shifted his feet and mumbled something that might have been, "It's fine."

"Does it hurt?" she asked.

His frown lessened, and he no longer had the posture of a man ready to run out the door.

"Not as much as it used to. If I'm in a rush and not careful, then yeah, it's not pleasant."

"How do you do it?"

"Not sure, to be honest. Same way I'm able to do anything. Demon magic."

*Right, of course.*

"Can you look like this permanently?" she asked, and immediately regretted it, not realizing how rude the question was until it left her mouth.

The lines of his face deepened again, and he focused his gaze on the window, not meeting her eyes. "No."

Whatever magic or ability he had cast was put in reverse, slow enough for Sam to watch. The ridged horns grew backwards above his ears, his wings unfurling and stretching to curl against his back. The tail reappeared, low and close to his leg, and his nails bent into a predatory shape.

He still wouldn't look at her, but there was an overall tension that eased as his demonic features reappeared.

"It's like...flexing a muscle," he said without prompting. "It takes energy and practice, otherwise it cramps, and that *does* hurt. But it's not my natural state, and I'll always return to this."

He indicated his body, his distaste apparent.

She cleared the dryness of her throat. "So, uh..."

"Yes?"

Sam desperately wanted to ask about the sex, why it had happened, if it would happen again, why he couldn't seem to control himself and neither could she—and instead, she skirted around the issue like a car at high speed narrowly avoiding a tree fallen in the road.

"Why was that...*Alp* thing here? What did it want?"

Spiros gave a half-shrug, a perfectly ordinary gesture that was strange on him. It made his wings rustle, giving off a noise like pieces of old leather rubbing against each other. He turned back to his work, and Sam didn't know if avoiding her gaze was intentional or a by-product.

"Old unfinished business?" He used the claw of the hammer

to pry off the bottom panel of her window, his brows furrowed as if the wood had personally wronged him. "Taking advantage of an opportune moment? Hunger pangs? Even I don't know how *Alpen* think. They're not human, and Earth isn't their natural habitat."

That only begged for more questions. Sam opened her mouth, but he glared at her, the pinched expression on his face stopping her.

"Look, Samara, I'll fix your lock, but that's it. We won't speak again. You need to forget I exist and go back to the life you were living. This isn't safe for you otherwise."

"Why?"

"Because *I'm* not safe for you."

"Is this about last night?"

His expression bordered on thunderous, dark clouds on the horizon warning her of what would happen if she persisted. But Sam weighed her options, and to her, the danger of not understanding the full situation weighed more heavily than the risk of his anger. She couldn't protect herself unless she knew what was happening, and Spiros was the only one who could explain it.

"Can you please just tell me what's happening?" Sam held out her hands plaintively. "If you won't, I'll find out another way, as you've seen."

"Samara," he growled in warning.

"Spiros," she responded, unimpressed.

His nostrils flared, and Sam considered if she'd gone too far, but then his wings drooped.

"I'm an incubus."

Silence followed as Sam waited for him to make a follow-up statement. He didn't.

"You're...an incubus."

"Yes. And yes, the kind you're thinking of."

"...Okay."

The dull look in his eyes was as flat as the inflection in his voice. "Incubi feed off human energy to survive in this world. Emotional energy, physical energy, psychic energy."

He took another breath, letting the implication linger before hammering it into place. "Sexual energy."

Sam rubbed the symbol on her hand, self-soothing rather than appeasing any true ache. She could almost feel his attention on the movement.

"Okay," she repeated. "How does it work?"

The window repairs entirely forgotten, Spiros leaned against the sill and faced her. "Incubi feed on humans, siphon their energy, during orgasm."

He pressed his lips together as if he didn't want to say more, but he continued. "And it has to be during orgasm. Incubi feeding and pleasure is so tied to the...orgasm of our prey, that we can't have either without it."

He grimaced, his discomfort obvious. "If we don't feed, we'll eventually starve. But before that, we go into something called an *epulum.* It's a kind of lust fever. A ravenous frenzy. We don't just lose control, though that is a big part of it. We also cause a sort of paralyzing fear over humans, enough so that they won't run, and then during the sex itself, the feeding act causes a limited amnesia."

His jaw clamped together so hard Sam worried he'd break teeth. "Or at least, it's supposed to. But you remember last night?"

Sam swallowed from both his focused gaze and the memory

of him pressing her down into the bed on which she now sat. "Up until I...yeah, the orgasm."

"You fell unconscious. That happens sometimes after intense feedings. And it was intense."

"Yeah, no kidding," Sam muttered before her brain could keep up with her mouth, but Spiros only raised a brow. "I remember things from Halloween, though it's not as clear. And I don't remember being afraid or paralyzed either time. At least, not from you."

She shivered at the memory of teeth and dark claws and green eyes. Sam couldn't imagine what other demons could possibly exist if the spectrum went from howling nightmare to long-haired dreamboat.

Sam had to press her lips together to keep from smiling. She couldn't imagine Spiros would appreciate her calling him that. In fact, he narrowed his eyes, as if he knew she was having thoughts he wouldn't like.

"Well," he spoke slowly, still watching her, "you don't seem to have the typical response to an incubus feeding. Clearly."

Sam decided she should try to move the conversation along before he burned holes in her with his eyes alone, and her tone was forcibly chipper as she said, "I actually thought I dreamed up the *Alp*, and that you were just some strange guy I brought home after the party."

His brows rose even higher.

"The *point,*" Sam emphasized in a hurry, "is that, while it's hazy, I remember some of it. I remember you talking about the Ouija board and watching over me, and then it's just... blank."

"What you don't remember," Spiros said, the words dragged out as if he was unwilling to speak them, "is what happened after.

Once the *Alp's* paralysis wore off, I attempted to wipe your mind—"

"You *what?!*"

"I've done it before. When you were a child and opened a portal that should have remained closed."

"I'm sorry? You can't be serious."

"Regardless, it didn't work." He steamrolled right over her perfectly reasonable concern. "I tried to wipe your memory, and instead, I had an *epulum.* I've fed on you twice now. I'm not sure how you remember any of it. I'm not sure about a lot of things."

His last sentence dropped off, as if he was speaking to himself rather than her.

"Why did you feed on me?"

His eyes widened. "I don't know."

"What the hell does that mean?"

"It means I don't know why I fed."

"On me?"

*"At all."*

His hollow-eyed expression was replaced by an undercurrent of real anger.

"I haven't fed for twenty-five years, and then you get attacked by an *Alp.*" He snarled as if the reminder of the creature's existence offended him. "I banished it just as I've banished so many others, and the next thing I know, my ability to wipe your memories failed, and I fed."

So, it was *her* fault, was it? Her temper flared to match his.

"And you showing up here today, to fix my window." She gestured angrily toward the broken lock. "Was that an excuse to try and make me forget a third time?"

"Even if I thought it would work, we're past the point it would help." His eyes narrowed. "Don't look at me like that, it was a safeguard measure. Knowing about demons would put a target on your back. It was protection."

"I didn't ask for that!"

His lips curved in a tired smile. "Some of the memory wipe worked, because we've already had this conversation. I'll tell you the same thing I told you then—you need to live your life and forget about all of this."

"I *can't.*" She stood and held out her arm, the pink lines etched in her flesh on display. "Not with this."

He ran a hand over his face. "I know."

The unspoken apology lingering in his words wasn't enough, but it was some kind of acknowledgement.

"I've been taking something that suppresses the feeding instinct," he eventually said.

He really did seem tired, from the sudden droop of his wings to the shadows under his eyes.

"It's how I've gone so long without an *epulum*. At first, I thought the formula failed. Now...I think it's connected to that." He nodded at her right hand.

Sam frowned and pulled her arm back, covering the mark with her sleeve.

"I need you to tell me who did that to you."

"You did."

Spiros shoved the screwdriver onto the windowsill with a sharp *slap,* the sound startling her. He turned to face her fully, wings slightly flared as he seemed to fill the room more than he had a moment ago.

"I am *not* fucking around."

Sam took an automatic step back.

"Tell me who did this." Spiros took a step forward, the movement graceful and threatening with no trace of the exhaustion she'd seen a moment ago. "Did they do it here or take you elsewhere? I don't care what they said or what promises they made, they're liars. Or did they do this to you to get to me?"

Sam backed up to the bedroom doorway but found she could go no further. Perhaps it was the intensity of his eyes that froze her on the threshold. She shook her head wordlessly, her voice fled, her heart racing in a panicked rhythm.

Spiros loomed over her, casting a literal shadow over her as he blocked out the light from the window. His gray eyes traced her features for a long moment until he eventually deflated.

"I'm sorry." He took a step back, giving her room to breathe.

She did, barely.

"But I need you to be honest. Your life depends on it."

Sam swallowed, the movement so difficult she nearly choked. "No one did this to me. I thought it was you, because it...it appeared the morning after Halloween. After the first time we—"

What happened that night took on a different meaning. She was marked. Branded with a message she still didn't understand, but one that felt possessive and trapping.

Sam held out her arm, allowing him to see the faint pink lines traced along the back of her hand, and she asked, "Do you know what this is?"

"Of course I do." He scowled at the mark, apparently no happier to see it than she was. "It's a demonic *signum*."

"And that is?"

"The mark that binds a demon to its new master."

Her stomach dropped, an invisible hand tight around her neck, her words breathless. "I'm not a demon."

*Was she?* She had no idea what it took to turn a man into a monster, the process or the prerequisites. She only knew the result, standing right in front of her. What if she were to become like him?

Her head spun. She would have to quit her job, not a great loss there. She'd have to stop hanging out with her friends, of which she didn't have many. But not being able to visit her mom and sister? Never seeing her family again? It was outrageous. *Unreasonable.* There had to be another way—

"Clearly," he said, deadpan and unamused as he returned to his spot by the window. "And I doubt you're going to become one. The ritual is a long, agonizing process, not something that can be done over the course of a single night."

He was quiet for a moment, fixating on his nails as they picked at the fallen wood chips on her sill. "And as far as I know, I am the only one to survive the full transformation."

Immediately, she longed to ask the things she knew he wouldn't want to answer. Who had done this to him? Why? He said he was the only one to survive, so did that mean there were others who hadn't?

What did this have to do with her and the Ouija board? Spiros had said she'd freed him, but from what?

Before she could gather the nerve to ask even one of her many questions, Spiros said, "The mark comes last, *after* demonification is complete. And it's carved into the skin; it doesn't just appear on its own. So, no. You're still human."

Sam sat on the edge of her bed slowly, as if afraid the mattress would disappear beneath her. "You're sure?"

He let out a light snort, as if he found her question funny.

"Trust me, I would sense it if you weren't." He paused, as if trying to choose his words carefully. "I'm very attuned to the presence of other demons. If there was a drop of demonic blood within you, I'd know."

And just like that, some of the roiling in her stomach calmed, the grip around her neck easing. She was curious how the ritual worked, but the topic seemed too large to broach with a casual, "how *does* one become a demon?" But Sam could start with something smaller.

"So," she began, trying not to sound too relieved. She didn't want to rub it in his face that she had managed to keep her humanity, and he hadn't. It would have felt wrong, like she was celebrating being saved from a housefire while he was still trapped inside. "The symbol must mean something else?"

"If it does, it's beyond me."

*Great.* All they knew was how much they didn't know. She supposed that was something.

Remembering what he'd said about why *signums* existed, Sam's gaze dropped to the symbol—not the one marring her flesh, but the one that marked his. It was exposed now that he'd removed his gloves, but even hidden away, she would know its shape. She could draw it in her sleep at this point, as she'd studied her own enough times to commit it to memory.

"You had a master?"

"Yes." His jaw worked. "No one owns me now, but they did once. And it wasn't just a mark of ownership, there was power behind it. Purpose. Such as when it would burn if I displeased my previous master. It's effective at punishing a demon who disobeys orders."

The blood drained from her face, not from her own predicament, but from his. Spiros seemed so strong and impenetrable. It was hard to imagine that he was vulnerable once. Forced to bow to others. Perhaps worse, given the nature of what kind of demon he was.

"So, you must understand, it's impossible that you have a

*signum,*" Spiros continued, practically accused, as if its appearance was her doing. "Which means you're probably right. Your *signum* must have a different meaning than mine. A different purpose."

His glare hardened, as did his words. He pushed away from the wall, and Sam rose in response, without thought, as if Spiros moving closer was some unspoken challenge she needed to meet. Plus, him looming over her as she sat on her bed would be a distracting reminder she didn't need.

"So I need to know if someone did this to you," he insisted, his voice low, almost a growl. "Was anyone else here? Do you have any missing time? Anything you can't explain?"

"Aside from what you did to me?"

His jaw flexed in irritation. "I said I was sorry."

"I don't think you did, actually."

His mouth opened, then shut, and then opened again. "I'm... sorry. I'm sorry for the feedings, and I'm sorry for...all of this."

"And for trying to take my memories?"

Spiros took another step forward, his mouth set in a grim line. "Some things shouldn't be remembered."

Sam prodded him in the chest since he insisted on standing so close. "That's not your decision to make."

"Of course it is."

Her anger flared, and so did the throbbing in her hand. She gripped it hard and rubbed her thumb along the stinging lines.

"What is it?" he asked, some of his annoyance lifting.

"It's this damn mark. *Signum*. Whatever. It looked like this at first." She continued to rub the smooth skin and the faint pink color, deceptively benign. "But after a week, it started to rise to the surface. And it got worse and worse, and well, you saw how it was last night. That was the first time it burned. I thought I was going to catch fire. And then after you—after last night, it faded away. Why did it do that? What does it mean?"

*Is it going to happen again?*

His response was slow to come, face blank but eyes gleaming with something she couldn't pinpoint before he turned back to the window. She glanced at his tail, hoping it would show a more honest assessment of his thoughts. The range of its movements was smaller now, but it still twitched sporadically, restlessly. Perhaps if she had practice reading him, she'd be able to know his moods simply by the rhythm of his tail.

"I have no idea what it means." Spiros picked up a flat-edged tool and began to smooth the rough edges of wood around where the lock used to be, once again avoiding Sam's gaze.

She expected that was the end of the conversation, until he added, "But I'm going to find out."

"Really?"

"I'm going to try."

She struggled to respond, taken aback. "Why?"

His movements slowed, and a few wood shavings drifted off the sill before he continued.

"While we might not know how it got there or exactly what it means in your case, that symbol is extremely dangerous." He shoved out the words in chunks with each push of the scraper. "And if it can be removed, all the better."

That wasn't what she expected, and the first hint of hope she'd felt in a long time struggled to the surface. She'd been so focused on why it was there that she hadn't imagined they could simply remove it or that Spiros would offer his help. And Sam didn't have the slightest idea how to grapple with either of those ideas.

"Could it have been the *Alp?*" Sam asked.

Maybe if the creature was the origin of the mark, it would bring them one step closer to removing its stain.

Spiros shook his head. "No. As far as I know, demons can't force a demonic transformation on humans. Some demons can possess them, sure, but not change them. The *Alp* wasn't looking for anything more than a meal."

The memory of the dark creature followed her like a bad acid trip, razor teeth lining its open maw like the petals of a poisonous flower. *Removing the mark will probably be easier than getting that face out of my head,* she thought.

Not that she would admit it aloud and let Spiros think he was right about the whole memory-erasure thing. He wasn't.

"It's not like an incubus, right?" she quietly asked. "It wasn't going to—"

"No, no, nothing like that." His words were quick and coated with a fine layer of discomfort. "The *Alpen* are dream-eaters. That's what they're called, anyway; they don't actually *eat* dreams, they feed off the mental energy of a human while they're dreaming."

His voice slipped into a practiced rhythm that was almost soothing, and Sam recognized it from her own past stints in lecture halls, though the subject here was decidedly more interesting than calculus.

"You've heard of sleep paralysis demons?"

She nodded.

"The phenomenon is most likely attributed to an *Alp* who didn't use enough venom to sedate their prey. The person wakes up, paralyzed, as a nightmarish figure stares down at them."

"Sounds terrible."

The corner of his mouth twitched. "Right. You woke at that stage."

He tapped the tool with his fingernails, mulling over his next words. "I know it was unpleasant, but it probably wouldn't have hurt you. The worst they do is turn dreams into nightmares. Still..."

Spiros returned to his work, scraping the wood a little harder than before.

"A demon's a demon."

The statement rubbed her wrong, like a cat being petted against the course of its fur.

"Are they, though? Are all demons the same?"

He paused briefly, and she waited, but he continued his work as if she hadn't spoken.

Sam pushed. "I mean, yes, you're a demon, but you're nothing like the *Alp—*"

"I'm exactly like the *Alp,*" he snapped. His movements were jerky as he screwed the new lock into the bottom of the window. "No, worse. At least it can't help what it is. I know better."

There was so much self-loathing in his tone that Sam struggled to find the right words. "But you can't control it. You said so yourself you don't know why it happened."

"Doesn't matter. I still did it." His tone brooked no argument, his fingers pressing into the wood so hard the window gave an ominous creak.

Spiros was going to damage her window even further if he kept it up, and Sam wracked her brain for a way to defuse the situation.

She returned to the bed and sat on its edge, closer to him than before. Despite his warnings, and despite her memories—both fuzzy and in graphic detail—it didn't bother her to be so close to him. It was difficult to see him as a demonic creature when everything he did allowed her a glimpse into something human.

His gaze remained fixed on his work, but something changed. His tail stopped its agitated staccato and paused before edging toward her, as if curious. At this close distance, its smooth texture was more obvious, and Sam wondered what it would be like to run her fingertips across its surface.

Her mark might not be burning, but there was still something under the surface that itched. A need to touch that she didn't experience often in her solitude. What would he do if she reached out and delicately placed her hand on his arm? Would he recoil? Run out of her apartment?

Succumb to a sudden, unnatural hunger?

Sam kept her hands to herself.

"What do we do?" she asked.

"*We* don't do anything," he responded. "*You* keep going, business as usual. I'm going to get this sorted out, but I can't do that and worry about you at the same time, so keep your head down and act as if nothing's changed."

"Are you *serious?*"

"Pretty damn serious."

"What if it gets bad again?"

"Then we deal with it."

"And by that, you mean..."

She gestured to her bed, and Spiros made a pinched expression that was awfully prudish for a sex demon.

"Yes." He turned back to the window and continued to drill the new lock into the notch where the old one had been seated.

It looked nearly done, and Sam's irritation faded, replaced by a tight knot in her ribcage. She couldn't do this alone, and she *would* be alone. Her mom could never know, she had no one to confide in, at work or outside of it, and the only person who understood her situation was the one telling her to pretend nothing was wrong.

Was she supposed to go back to paying bills, fighting traffic, and making appointments until the next time the mark burned?

"When?"

"When what?" he asked, not looking up.

"When is it going to happen again?"

The hard lines of his shoulders went rigid. "We don't know it will."

"But if it does?"

"I don't know."

"Another month?" she asked. "Longer? Shorter?"

"I don't *know.*"

"Is it time-based? Or aggravated by something else? What triggers it?"

*"I said I don't—"*

He sucked in a breath, short and harsh. His tail, which Sam expected to lash angrily, curled tightly around his leg, like an animal seeking comfort.

Her stomach churned, but she had to push. Having answers was all she had, a way to feel like she wasn't waiting in the dark for something to snatch her in its latching jaws.

"Well..." she tried, more gently this time. "How often did you feed before?"

Spiros paused, and then he gathered up his tools and placed them back in his kit. Sam hadn't realized he was finished.

When he spoke, she strained to catch the soft words.

"At the beginning, when the demonic aspects were taking hold, I could go a month without feeding. The more I fed, the less human I became, and the more that time shortened."

Sam didn't like where this was going, but the next question was inevitable. "And when you became a full demon?"

"A week."

A *week?* That was all?

"But you're not a demon, your *signum* might be something completely different." He spoke as if she'd had a panicked outburst rather than remained frozen on the edge of the bed. "We don't know if they're even related."

"They seem pretty damn related." Sam pressed her lips together in a smile that felt jagged and wrong. "The pain only left after we—after you fed on me. And it wasn't just the pain, or the burning. You know that, right? You know it was more than that?"

There was a soft sadness in his eyes, an understanding of what she wasn't saying. The all-consuming need, the destructive inferno of obsession, the cataclysmic landslide of desire. The storm had only calmed after he'd broken her apart and emptied her clean.

Her hands shook, her carefully crafted composure slipping under the weight of realization. This was her life now.

"I know," he said quietly. "I know."

In that moment, all Sam wanted to do was reach out and touch him. Take some little human comfort for herself, even if he wasn't human and even if touch was the last thing either of them probably wanted. She still ached for him to cross the room and embrace her, if only for a moment so she wouldn't feel so *alone.*

But he wasn't going to do that, and Sam wasn't going to ask.

Sam nodded. She would survive this. And if she didn't, well, then she wouldn't be around to worry.

She fixed her expression in calm surrender, the composure set in place, and she rose to her feet. "Thank you for fixing my window. You didn't have to do that."

"Yeah, I did," he said. There was a hint of a tiny smile. "Was nice to use these hands to fix something, for once. Where's your phone?"

"What?"

"Your cell phone. Let me see it."

With a frown, Sam patted her pockets and pulled out her phone, a fractional hesitation before she handed it over.

Spiros stared at the screen and then at her blankly. "Unlock it. Please?"

Sam entered the passcode, and Spiros tapped the screen a few times before returning it.

"There."

Sam examined the screen and found the contact list open.

"If you need me, for whatever reason? Call."

Sam narrowed her eyes. "You have a phone."

"Yes. I have a phone."

"Do you have a car?"

She was rewarded with a sour expression.

"I have wings."

"Wait, you can actually *fly*?"

"Did you think these were just for show?"

"Kind of. Do you live in a house?"

He rolled his eyes and tucked the toolkit and jacket under his arm, leaving her standing in her bedroom, phone in hand and questions still on her tongue.

She hurried after him, trailing him to the front door like a duckling left behind by its mother. "A houseboat? A cabin? You look like a cabin guy."

He said nothing and paused before her front door.

Sam watched as his wings, tail, and horns retracted into his body, wincing at the sound of grinding bones and sliding skin.

There were two holes at the back of his shirt, sewn rather than ripped, and he slid the jacket over his shoulders to hide the bare skin of his back. He tugged on his gloves, and the veneer was complete. He could have been anyone walking the downtown streets, a local or a seasoned tourist practiced at the art of blending in.

Spiros stared for so long that her smile faded, drifting into nothingness as if she'd performed a transformation of her own.

"You call me, day or night, if something happens—including if the *signum* hurts again. Got it?"

"Yeah. Got it."

She didn't appreciate being bossed around by the demon version of IT, but the idea of him being available in an emergency was...nice.

He hesitated for the briefest moment, as if wanting to give additional instruction, but he said nothing. Spiros opened the door, crossed the threshold, and disappeared around the corner into the hallway.

Sam watched his progression, leaning around her doorway to do so, and she wasn't the only one. Mr. Morris's beady eyes glanced between her and Spiros's retreating figure, his mouth puckered into a suspicious frown.

She shut the door in a hurry.

The smooth weight in her hand drew her attention, and she unlocked her phone and brought up the contact list again. A new entry was added. A single name, one that left a trace of apprehension and a small crumb of comfort.

*Ash.*

## CHAPTER NINE

# SAM

MID-DECEMBER. A MONTH AND A HALF SINCE Halloween. Two weeks since Spiros had fixed Sam's window, and there had been no sign of horn or hide since.

Despite the strange, occultic tilt to her life, bills still had to be paid, and work quotas had to be filled. There was nothing quite like the mundanity of an office to ground her in reality, but it also placed a disconnected filter over her perception. The office was a liminal space, her coworkers were strangers, and the commute through drizzle and overcast skies was dreamlike.

Only at home did she feel on solid ground. Sam didn't know why that was; all things strange and terrifying had occurred in her apartment, at least recently. And yet she felt more real there than anywhere else.

Sadly, matters of existential crisis didn't stop her team manager from delegating mandatory overtime during the fast-approaching holiday season. That's how she found herself at the six o'clock hour, staring blankly at her monitor when she preferred to be on her couch, Monster curled next to her legs as she sipped something smooth and warm.

But there were holiday gifts to consider, and her lease ended soon with an unspoken promise that rent would rise again. She would be pushed out of the city at the current rate of inflation, but the thought of moving back to Spokane was as appealing as laying out in traffic.

Naked.

Leaning an elbow on her desk, Sam rubbed her temple. She didn't have a headache, yet, but there was a mounting pressure that had increased throughout the day, along with an ache elsewhere she didn't want to think about. Nor would she acknowledge the burning on the back of her hand.

Two weeks since Spiros had been to her apartment, which meant two weeks since he'd fed on her. After Halloween, she'd been granted a month's reprieve before the mark began to burn, and now that time had been halved.

Did Spiros feel it too? A deep hunger pang, a desire to hunt down his food source and feed? And why was she forced to meet him with the same heady need? What kind of fucked up symbiosis made the food *crave* to be eaten?

Studying demonic habits and feeding cycles might have been fascinating if Sam wasn't slated to be the next meal.

She shivered even though the office was at a perfectly unoffensive temperature. If only there were more time. To learn, to adjust, to adapt—but there was no negotiating with the throb in her hand.

To make matters worse, she wouldn't be allowed to retreat after her shift and nurse her anxiety in the seclusion of her apartment. Stacey was throwing yet another office party—this time at her house—and Sam had accepted the invite at a time when things had been quiet. She hadn't expected to have to deal with her new, problematic "condition" until around Christmas.

It was like trying to coordinate around a menstrual cycle from Hell. Literally.

But it wasn't that bad *yet.* She could still go to the party. *Should* go to the party. Managers took notice of these things, *make an effort,* and all that. Sam needed a significant raise to keep up with skyrocketing costs in Seattle. Moving back home was unappealing to any adult who'd escaped the confines of childhood, but for Sam, it was impossible while a certain demon encroached on her life...and her body.

Not that Sam couldn't imagine her mother cooing and doting over Spiros, at the pretty picture he painted when he wore his human face, ignorant of what truly lay beneath.

No, that was a situation Sam would avoid at all costs, which meant biting the bullet and going to the damned party. She'd stop by, socialize just long enough to stick in anyone's vague memory of the party, and then get out. These things were bad enough, but being horny and miserable at her boss's house would make Sam seriously consider chopping off her own hand. It couldn't punish her body if there was no body it connected to.

*At least there will be alcohol.*

And with that thought, Sam shut off her workstation, clocked out, and exited the silent office at a brisk pace.

The night bit at any part of exposed skin, and Sam stuck her hands into her pockets, pulling her peacoat around her waist. It was the kind of weather that called for a proper winter jacket, not whatever Sam had grabbed out of her closet, and her long, heavy skirt was a poor substitute for thick pants. But that morning, as soon as she'd slipped on her nice pair of office slacks, she'd known they were a bust. The crotch seam, completely unnoticeable before, was suddenly a line of pressure against her oversensitive clit, making her double over with a gasp.

Sam had been lucky enough to find an old skirt buried in one of her storage boxes. Even if she wanted to risk the pants now, as soon as she stepped foot in her apartment, the party would be nothing but a distant, well-intentioned nonevent.

It was shockingly cold, even for Seattle, near the zero-degree mark as a polar vortex moved over the region. The parking garage protected her car from the worst of it, but even underground, she felt the Arctic chill. Sam stuffed herself into the small car, but the engine struggled to turn over, and the metal frame creaked ominously with each shift of weight. The wheels, too, seemed unhappy with each turn of the steering wheel, having to be coaxed into obeying.

With barely any traffic, Sam was parked near Stacey's townhouse within ten minutes. Street parking was hard to find, and by the time she made it to the front stoop, her fingers were numb to the press of the doorbell.

The sound of muffled music came from inside the classic brownstone, warm and distant. A thatch welcome mat announced that *Love Makes Its Home Inside,* and the maple trees that stood close scratched against the brick as if asking to be let inside. Her breath fogged like the bellows of a steam engine, or the exhale of an ancient dragon.

Or perhaps, a demon.

The hair on the nape of her neck prickled, a harsh sensation like a tiger was baring its teeth just inches away.

She spun, but the street remained devoid of life. Sam rubbed the back of her neck, and her hand flared hot under the fingerless glove. Her finger bones ached, her tendons engulfed like twine on fire.

The door swung open and Sam jumped. A hand shot out and

grabbed her arm before she could topple down the steps. Green eyes met her under a mop of blond hair.

"Sorry," Davin said with a flash of white teeth. "Didn't mean to startle you."

Sam pantomimed something like a smile, though it might have been a baring of teeth.

"Hope I'm not late," she replied through the tight gesture. "Just finished up at the office."

His hand lingered on her arm longer than he had a right to. He finally released her, pressed his back to the door, and held it open. "You're right on time."

His obstructive position meant she would have to squeeze past him over the threshold, and she considered simply standing there until he moved. Why couldn't he just hold the door open like a normal human being?

Davin didn't budge, so she shuffled past him, managing not to step on his feet, though all things considered, maybe she should have.

"Can I take your coat?"

*No.*

"Yes."

Sam allowed him to take the coat. He folded it over a nearby chair and then gave her a cheerful nod and disappeared into the crowd.

Maybe this office party wouldn't be as humiliating as the last one.

The air inside was thick from the heat of pressed bodies and the brick fireplace licking around fake logs. The stifling space did nothing to improve Sam's mood or distract her from her burning hand. It wasn't only the mark; her skin was flushed and warm, overheated from more than just the cold.

After greeting a few coworkers and making sure Stacey spotted her—Sam was trying, *goddamnit*—she made a beeline for the side table. She'd spotted the wine bottles earlier, a life preserver after being dumped overboard.

As soon as she made it to the table, she froze. Theresa sat in an armchair nearby, her gaze fixed on the fire while also a thousand miles away.

"Hey, Theresa."

The other woman didn't notice Sam at first, and then she blinked and looked up, giving a delayed smile that felt perfunctory.

"Sam, hi. You made it."

"Yeah," she said, far less interested in the party than whatever was going on right in front of her.

Theresa's hair had dulled, and some of the coiled strands hung loose from her hair tie, absent its usual shiny, tight gloss. Bags hung beneath her eyes, and she seemed older in a way that was hard to quantify in years.

"That's good." Theresa returned her attention to the fire, as if she'd already forgotten Sam was there.

"Are you...okay?"

"Sure," Theresa said so quickly that it sounded like a preprogrammed response from a machine. "Just tired. Holidays, you know?"

"Yeah." Sam eyed the crowd. "I saw Davin."

Theresa stiffened, her shoulders pulled in a defensive position as her jaw tightened, and then she relaxed as if she hadn't just performed the full body equivalent of a clenched fist. "Oh? I haven't seen him."

She said nothing else, and Sam guessed she would say nothing more, her dark brown eyes fixed on the flickering flames. Sam imagined she could see them dancing within their depths.

"I'll see you around, then," Sam said, her tone even and normal, as if this was another day at the office.

"Course. I'll see you later, Sam."

Sam left her there, vacant-eyed and staring at the fire. She frowned all the way to the wine table. Maybe she should keep an eye on Theresa during the workday. A part of her wanted to go back, sit down next to her, and ask what was wrong. But Sam didn't know how. She'd never been good at that kind of thing, and she had her own problems to deal with.

She poured herself a generous amount of wine from the first bottle she grabbed, the burn sliding down her throat distracting her from the one consuming her hand. Soon enough, there was a pleasant heat rather than a scorching one. Even the colors of the room seemed warmer, the flicker of firelight reflecting off the Brooklyn-inspired brickwork, dousing everything in hues of orange and yellow.

Sam didn't know if it was the wine, the warmth, or the mark, but the heavy pressure between her legs grew steadily worse. Unexpected arousal would have been annoying on a typical day, and she would have left the party early to distract herself with ice cream and a show. Instead, she found herself fleeing to the upstairs bathroom and locking the door with frightened unsteadiness.

The gentle burn had risen into a tantalizing fire, covering her skin in pinpricks of heat and sweat. Her heart raced a frantic rhythm, her hands trembled so hard she had to abandon the wineglass, and every time her thighs rubbed together, she had to breathe deeply through her nose.

To her knowledge, no one had spotted her slinking upstairs,

but she still triple-checked the lock. The heat was smothering, and she hiked up her skirt as she laid on the cold tile, curled into a small ball like a child being surrounded by schoolyard bullies.

Sam didn't want to do this. She did *not* want to do this. But the knowledge that relief was only a few minutes away was irresistible, and if she was quiet, no one would know.

Squeezing her eyes tight, Sam slipped her hand under her skirt and into her underwear. Humiliation burned her eyes at the feel of her own wetness, fabric soaked to the point of ruin, and her clit was swollen past anything resembling normal.

She didn't want to think of anything at all, tried to keep her mind carefully blank, but the images slipped through, supplied with tactile memories of warm skin and solid muscle. A smell of pine and earth, gray eyes that were cold in the darkness, but shone in the light of day, like a winter lake in the morning sun.

Her memories might be overwhelming from the second feeding and mostly absent from the first, but there were specific details she couldn't forget. The unusual heat of his skin, smooth over the parts of him that were human, rough where they weren't.

The ache ran deep, far deeper than she could ever reach; it split her in half, a thunderbolt out of the blue, and she gritted her teeth in a pained moan. She worked herself with her fingers, her enflamed flesh not needing much encouragement. She would last only a few more seconds.

Sam curled her toes. She was right on the cusp—until she hit a plateau. A ceiling blocked her from reaching the peak, and she could go no further.

Crying out in frustration, she jerked her hand away, but the pressure was unrelenting and edged toward pain rather than pleasure. The mark throbbed in time with her heartbeat as if to show it belonged there, as much a part of her body as any organ.

She tried to stand once, twice, and on the third try, she gained her feet, hoisting her weight against the sink so she wouldn't fall. Trembling so much the water splashed around the sink, she washed her hands and splashed cold water on her face. Even the cold, wet washcloth to the back of her neck—a tried and true method to knock her out of an anxiety loop—didn't help.

Nothing helped. Her body was afire, pulsing with a primal fury, denied what it sought and willing to take out its vengeance on her. She pulled her phone from her pocket, fumbled it, unlocked it, opened her contact list, and pulled up the "A" names.

She froze. And slowly put down the phone.

She couldn't do it. Letting Spiros see her like this was too much. It was mortifying. *Humiliating.* Even though she was sure he would understand—that she had no control, that she didn't want this—she couldn't face it. Face *him.* Sam just wanted to be back in her apartment, where she would be comfortable and safe. Maybe if she was home, the thought of calling him wouldn't be so daunting.

*No. I can handle this on my own. Drive home, deal with it there. Don't tell him.*

It was the mantra she played in her mind over and over as she made herself presentable, phone placed back in her pocket with heavy skirt smoothed over. She did what she could for her frayed hair and wrinkled jacket, wanting to leave no trace of what she'd been doing in her boss's bathroom.

Her first step to the door faltered, and she grabbed onto the nearby towel rack, knees threatening to buckle as her cunt tightened around nothing, empty and aching for what wasn't there.

Sam closed her eyes and took several calming breaths; the results were a whimper more than breathing.

*Focus.* One thing before another. Make it out of the bathroom. Worry about what comes later.

Logical in theory, not so much in practice. Sam had to brace against the wall like a drunk, dragging herself along until she came to the door, shoes scraping against the veined marble tiles.

She fumbled for the keys in her other pocket to make sure they were there but didn't take them out—if she dropped them now, that would be the end of her. Getting up from the floor was not something she could achieve a second time.

Unlocking the door, Sam eased it open and leaned on it like an old friend as she checked the hallway. Empty, and from the noise coming up the stairs, the party had proceeded without her. If her luck held, she could slip out unseen before anyone, perhaps rightly, took her keys.

Sam shuffled along the wall like a zombie or a stabbing victim rather than a human being. Each step brought a fresh wave of painful heat and torturous throbbing. Sweat beaded her skin, wetting her hair to her forehead and causing her clothes to stick.

She made it halfway down the hall before she had to stop, most of her weight supported by the wall.

Sam didn't know what to do. Even if she made it to the stairs, she could easily envision herself tumbling down them from a single misstep. And her *hand,* the heat scorched with unrelenting fury up her arm like a field of chaff catching fire.

She was going to burn.

As Sam's knees gave out beneath her, a hand curled around her arm and yanked her sideways, dragging her into darkness.

CHAPTER TEN

# SAM

SHOVED AGAINST THE SURFACE OF THE CLOSED DOOR, Sam couldn't move. Carved grooves of wood dug into her back, and a cry would have left her mouth if it hadn't been covered by something heavy and warm.

Shadows draped the room with the exception of moonlight filtering through the open window, but even if plunged in total darkness, she would have known who had taken ahold of her. The knowledge thrummed deep in her bones, the scent of pine and earth washing over her exaggerated senses.

Spiros glared, eyes dark and lips bared in a silent snarl. Snow dusted his hair and the shoulders of his windbreaker. His smooth, reptilian tail flickered behind him in constant agitation. Snowflakes continued to drift into the room, which seemed to be a wood paneled reading study, books lining the shelves muting the sound of voices and music from below. There was a feeling of complete isolation, as if they were adjacent to the world but not truly in it.

"Why didn't you *call me?*"

Sam's body was a creature separated from her control,

shivering and trembling as she tried to press closer to him. The cold air reaching its tendrils from outside was a relief against her heated skin, but it was overwhelmed by the wave of want that threatened to drown her in the riptide.

Spiros removed his hand so she could speak, but Sam had no words to share. When she started to slide down the wood, he grabbed both her arms and pushed her back against the closed door.

Fury radiated from the demon, but Sam didn't care. She was barely a person, a simple thing of balled flesh that forgot how to beg, so it trembled with a need that bordered on grief.

He'd known to come to her. He always knew. And some bestial part of her reveled in the knowledge he would come running.

"I m-made it worse," she said through hitched breaths. "So much worse. Didn't th-think."

Sam closed her eyes; it didn't help much, but it put a filter on at least one of her senses, so she didn't feel so alien in her own skin.

"Please. I need...please..." She babbled, desperate and afraid and yearning, the ache so deep she feared it would split her in two. "Please...I'm sorry..."

"Okay." His rough edges were gone, a kind of tired defeat taking their place. "Okay."

Pulling back only far enough to reach the front of his trousers, he unbuckled his belt and yanked down the zipper. His bulge was prominent and eager, a reaction Sam knew by now was solely tied to his hunger, but it didn't matter. Like a trained response, saliva flooded her mouth at the sound of his belt unbuckling, and her muscles coiled like a predator about to spring on its prey if it made the wrong move.

She was the prey in this hierarchy, the meal to be consumed, but reluctance belonged only to him. Sam was impatient, eager, and utterly unlike herself. Only a small part of her rational forebrain returned when Spiros pulled himself from his trousers.

She'd only gotten glimpses of his body during the prior feedings, and time and fuzzy recollection had convinced her what she remembered was wrong.

His cock was only human in the barest sense of its shape. Ridges lined the underside, the head was tapered, and there was a soft bulge at the base of the shaft. But it was the sheer size of him that made her pause with the certainty that what she craved could kill her. His equipment was clearly not meant to involve a human body.

But even as her mind balked, her body warmed, and she took him in her hands with a confidence she didn't recognize.

Before she could test that confidence, Spiros grabbed her around the thighs and lifted. Sam yelped and wrapped her legs around his waist, but his hands under her legs kept her from falling.

He rucked up her heavy skirt, bunching it around her hips. Sam gripped his shoulders tight, trying to find an anchor to keep her from floating away. She took a shuddering breath and braced her head against the door as the tip of his cock nudged between her labia. He hadn't bothered to remove her underwear; he simply pulled it aside.

He began to push, and impossibly, Sam's body accommodated. The stretch of her entrance was a tight pressure that stole her breath, the ridges of his cock strumming along her inner walls like a guitarist plucking at strings.

Spiros eased inside as her body opened to him with unnatural obedience. She was soaking wet, dripping around this massive intrusion, but her lubrication still couldn't explain how he fit inside her without tearing her apart.

Sam didn't care how it worked, only that it did. The relief as his hips finally met hers, the bulb at the base snug against her entrance, was enormous. Her eyes burned and tears ruined her vision, but she was too relieved, too grateful, to feel any humiliation.

Spiros dipped close, his thumb tracing over the lingering tears, tender. Surprising. A shudder rippled down her spine, and he groaned as her body gripped him with impatience.

"I know," he mumbled into her ear. "I know."

When he started to move, it was slow, gentle, and a part of Sam responded. Desperate for a careful touch, to be held, kissed—a connection to illuminate the dark and show she wasn't alone.

But the other part of her, the part that had hijacked her life and turned it into a bizarre funhouse of horror, won in the end. Her legs flexed around his waist, and she whimpered the words that weren't a pitiful entreaty but a demand for completion, even if ruin was the result.

*"Fuck me. Please."*

He pulled Sam from the door, gripped her ass, and slammed her against the wall next to the doorframe.

Her cry was short-lived since his rolling hips stole her breath away, each thrust driving deeper with purposeful fury. She'd goaded him into this, and Sam reveled in the punishment.

She wasn't going to last long, and she could actually feel the pull of it, something vital trickling from her to him. Sex used to be like giving a piece of herself away, never to get it back and be made whole again, but this was different. What she gave away would be replenished after a good sleep, and it wasn't something he took in careless boredom or simple pleasure.

He needed this for survival. He needed her to *live.*

The heady sensation of holding his life within her hands pushed her closer to the edge, but as she started to tighten, Spiros froze in jarring stillness.

Sam growled at the loss of movement, but the noise was cut short as Spiros clamped a hand over her mouth again. She squirmed, her teeth bared against his palm, but his strength restrained her with ease.

Distant footsteps thudded on the second-floor landing only a few feet on the other side of the wall. The possibility of being caught should have been at the forefront of her mind, but the only thing that occupied her world was the heavy stretch of him spreading her open.

Her body, a willful creature, ground her hips against his, seeking any relief she could.

He ignored it, until she squeezed around him in an attempt to milk him on the spot. His breath hitched like a punch to the gut, and Spiros pressed hard against her, delivering a warning glare as he trapped her between his pelvis and the wall.

The footsteps moved past the room, and the bathroom door closed.

Aware enough to know they would have to wait until the occupied bathroom was vacated, Sam tried to remain still, but her traitorous body was a live wire, shivering with an unending current.

Spiros's expression was as taut as a rubber band pulled beyond its breaking point, and Sam wanted to see the snap.

But he had succeeded in restraining her so tightly there wasn't room to move, so she got creative, and dragged her tongue along the flat of his palm. He tasted of salt and skin, with a hint of some kind of earthen spice.

Spiros moved his palm away. Before she could feel bereft, his hand returned—not his palm, but his fingers—and he pressed them between her parted lips.

Sam took them greedily, closing her mouth around his middle and forefinger. The tips of his nails scraped against her tongue, the pointed pressure a wonderful distraction.

He focused intensely on her face as her tongue swirled languid around his fingers. She wanted more of this, more of him in her mouth, heavy on her tongue, an impossible feat given he was still embedded inside her.

But if his hunger was a demonic need, hers was insatiably human, and she closed her eyes against the aching intrusion through two points of her body. The way he filled her was like a glass close to spilling over the brim, yet nowhere enough to fill the bottomless depths.

The nails of his other hand dug into her hip as he buried his nose in her hair, inhaling deeply. The planes of his body were pressed so tight against Sam that she could feel every breath and heartbeat.

The intensity of the moment was nearly surreal as they balanced on the edge, waiting to see who would snap first.

What could have been an eternity later, the bathroom door finally opened, followed by footsteps retreating down the hallway. The owner of those footsteps must have been out of earshot because Spiros pulled back and plunged forward, hard and without warning.

Any noise Sam could make choked around his fingers, and when he removed them, she cried out at the loss. But now Spiros had access to both of his hands, and he adjusted his grip on her thighs and thrust up into her. Something sinewy and strong wrapped around her ankle, his tail holding her tight like a binding shackle.

Each plunge drove Sam closer to the edge at a maddeningly fast tilt. He slowed his pace, rolling his hips and grinding against her clit with purpose. His harsh breath warmed her cheek, his claws indenting her skin with what would later become bruises.

Sam clenched so hard she was sure one of them would break, probably her. In the next breath, the wave slammed against shore, leaving her boneless in its wake. Sparks ignited along her nerves followed by a backlash of bliss.

Her climax dragged her across its surface, each energetic pulse followed by another, and every time she thought it was over, another throb from the base of his cock would take her back to that same dizzying height. She was stretched impossibly open, and her pelvic and abdominal muscles seized, like a contraction, but there was no pain, only a silent plea for it to never end.

Spiros's hand covering her mouth was the only thing that prevented her screams from ringing through the house, but she made plenty of hushed noises as she writhed. Spiros was oddly quiet and motionless. The only signs of his slipping control were his trembling fingers and his forehead braced against hers.

Her thoughts were scattered to the wind; she wasn't thinking when she leaned forward, and her nose bumped against his.

Spiros tensed, then pulled away.

Sam pretended it didn't feel like a slap to the face.

Avoiding her eyes, he gripped the base of his shaft and tried to remove himself. He couldn't. He tried again, and then a third time, before finally meeting her gaze with what looked like concern. Probably wishful thinking on her part.

"Does it hurt?" he asked, and by *it* she guessed he meant the bulb at the base of his cock that currently stuck them together. It didn't seem to be all the way inside, and she couldn't imagine how it would feel if it was.

"Feels...weird."

Her words came out brittle, and his jaw clenched hard enough for the muscles to bunch.

"Okay, just relax. Breathe. I think it's almost out."

He sounded unsure but not surprised, and she realized she had been unconscious and unaware for this part before. The longer he stayed inside, stretched her out, the more the strange feeling passed, leaving a pleasant warmth. She wanted to move against it, see how it would feel, but she didn't think he would appreciate that. It meant nothing to either of them.

Right?

Delicately, inch by stubborn inch, Spiros managed to pull himself out. With one arm around Sam, he supported her so she wouldn't fall.

She might be lucid, but her body was laden with satisfaction that was too heavy to be ordinary post-sex bliss. By the time he set her down on her own two feet, the embarrassment of what she'd done, what she'd *begged* him to do, was almost too much to swallow.

Come leaked out of her, further ruining her underwear, adding to the feeling of discomfort and uncleanliness.

"Can you walk?" Despite his unreadable mask in place, he hovered over her, watching her.

She wanted to shrug him off, tell him to leave now that their business was concluded.

"Yes," she mumbled.

Her purse was on the ground, left abandoned in her desperation to be fucked like a goddamn animal, and she teetered toward the bag.

Spiros moved forward, but Sam ignored him and snatched up her purse. She didn't want his help. Didn't need it. The deed was done, so why was he still here?

"I tried to take as little as possible." His shoulders were hunched and his tail drooped. "You should be able to drive home without issue."

"Thanks."

She hooked the strap over her shoulder, her bones now hollowed instead of glowing with post-orgasmic bliss. She needed to get out of this room, this goddamn house, and be anywhere else.

Her jaw clenched as if that would keep the rest of her intact, Sam opened the door and surveyed the hall. No one was there, and she escaped to the privacy of the bathroom, not giving a backwards glance to the demon.

He'd gotten what he needed, and so had she. Anything more would spoil the meal and lead to indigestion.

## CHAPTER ELEVEN

# SAM

WITH A HAPHAZARD BLEND OF WARM WATER AND tissues, Sam tried to erase the evidence as best she could.

Her underwear was ruined to the point where only a washing machine could save it, so she stripped it off, rinsed and wrung it dry, and balled the fabric into her purse. This was her first time slinking out of a party with her panties tucked out of sight, but here she was doing it within spitting distance of turning forty.

Sam caught her reflection in the mirror. Hair disheveled, cheeks flushed, and eyes glazed, she looked either high, stoned, or like she'd had a quickie with a coworker in the closet.

After rinsing her face and attempting to put her hair into a sensible ponytail, she left the bathroom and crept toward the landing like a burglar who had almost gotten away with it. Sam's legs still tingled but they seemed steady, and she hoped they remained that way. Cracking her head open on the stairs would be unfortunate.

Sam took a breath and plunged down the steps at a breakneck pace. Her focus on the front door, she weaved through the huddle of bodies and silently begged the universe to give her a reprieve for once in her goddamn life.

*"Wandern!"*

She grabbed her coat off the chair, nearly tipping it over in her haste to get out before the familiar voice could—

"Hey! You leaving already?"

Like a consequence yet to be reaped, Davin hovered at her elbow, denying her any peace. It felt like there was a neon sign over her head announcing she'd just been shamelessly fucked against a wall in the drawing room. The thought of Davin knowing what she'd done made her skin scrawl.

"Yeah," she said. "Not feeling great."

*Take the goddamn hint.*

"Ah, sorry to hear that." He moved forward, as if intentionally blocking her only escape. "Do you need anything? Maybe a ride back to your place? I could take you, no problem."

"No." The door was so close Sam could almost feel the winter chill that would signal her freedom. "Thank you. I'm fine."

She moved past him, forcing him to step aside or be bowled over.

"You don't look fine."

Sam's hand froze where it almost touched the handle. She turned. "What does that mean?"

Davin blinked. "I, uh, didn't mean anything. But let's be honest, you drink at these things sometimes, and I—"

"Yeah. I do. And frankly, that's none of your business, Davin."

"Whoa." He put up his palms. "Sorry, Sam. I just worry."

"Well, don't."

"Jesus, okay."

He ran a hand through his hair, attempting to smooth it, but all it did was ruffle the blond strands further. "I don't know why you brush me off when I'm trying to be nice—"

She dug her nails into her purse to keep them from digging into his face. "Since you can't seem to take a hint, I'll put it in clear terms to avoid any future confusion."

Sam leaned forward.

"Fuck. Off."

She realized too late the background noise of the party had died a quiet death. People were turned toward her, silent in surprise or their faces pinched in vindication of some imaginary proof they had against her. One of those heads was full of bright red hair the same perky color as Stacey's.

*"Shit,"* Sam muttered then grabbed the door handle and yanked it open.

Freezing air struck her, flurries stinging her cheeks, but she didn't slow her pace. She fumbled for her car keys, hands clumsy and shaking. By the time she unlocked the door and collapsed inside, her fingers had gone numb.

She turned her heat on full blast and rested her forehead against the steering wheel.

Why had she done that? Why had she done any of it? And more importantly, how was she going to show her face at work?

Sam's stomach curdled. Most importantly, *right.* As if her job was the true fundamental fuck up here. She had either overestimated herself, or underestimated what it would actually mean to go through this...two, three, *four* times a *month?*

Huddling against the wheel, Sam let a minute pass. Then, two minutes. She was parked far enough from her boss's house that no one should stumble upon her car, even if they could see past the fogged windows. The soft patter of snowflakes against the windshield was soothing, but it was also building up, and Sam knew she should leave before the winter storm arrived in full force.

She didn't look forward to stewing at home, either. Misery, company, and all that.

Exhaustion settled into her bones, and it would be a simple thing to close her eyes and float away. It was comfortable now, the air shaken free of the chill. The lull of the car engine and the soft rush of the heater could sing her to sleep—

Something tapped at the window next to her head, and she bolted upright, bracing for a cop to write her up for sleeping in her car, or worse, Davin wanting to continue the confrontation. She found it was neither of those things.

Even through the fogged glass, Sam recognized the silhouette, altered from its typical intimidating shape.

She yanked the button to roll down the window. The glass slid with an ominous creak from the temperature difference.

Spiros greeted her with an unhappy frown, his hands deep in his jacket pockets, his shoulders hunched against the chill. His wings, tail, and horns were conspicuously absent, his ears normal and round. Even though she couldn't see his teeth, they would be blunt and absent of their predatory nature. His human appearance was flawless, but seeing him in public so exposed sent her heart racing.

"What are you doing here?"

Beyond the deepening of his frown, he didn't react.

"Was going to ask you the same." Spiros glanced down the empty street, slow to meet her eyes again. "I waited to make sure you left. That there were no complications," he added. "The after-effects can be...wearing."

She wondered how good his hearing was, and how much he'd heard of her lost temper. By the furrowed tilt of his brow, quite a bit. Sam leaned against the headrest and released a breath.

"I don't know what I'm doing," she admitted.

"Why don't you start by letting me drive you home?"

She fixed him with a stare, but no comedic punchline followed.

"You...can drive?"

"Believe it or not, folks notice when demons go flying around their city in broad daylight. Yeah, I know how to drive."

She frowned. "I thought you said you didn't have a car. Because, you know, the wings?"

He didn't roll his eyes, but he exhaled sharply, white plumes billowing from his mouth. An irritated dragon being asked too many questions by a thieving hobbit.

"Car by day, flying by night. Does that satisfy your curiosity?"

Not even close, but the snow drifted heavier now, catching in his hair and leaving a fine layer of white on his shoulders. She wondered if he felt the cold like she did, or if demons were immune to that kind of thing. Yet another question she would have to file away under *things I don't know about Ashley Kane Spiros.*

"Okay, Spiros," she said. "Have at it."

Why not? Her night was already full of bad decisions, and she hated driving in the snow.

Sam opened the door and got out, skirting around the demon and the front of the car to reach the passenger side. Even a few seconds outside the comfort of her heater was a shock, the frigid fingers of winter clawing at any piece of exposed skin.

Spiros watched her, his hand on the frame of the door as he waited for her to get inside. He didn't take the driver's seat until she shut the passenger door, and Sam's tiny car creaked with the additional weight as he climbed inside.

It was a tight fit, especially for him, and Spiros had to move the seat back to accommodate his longer legs. At least with the car running it had heated nicely, but the offset was having to share the same air. His scent wasn't the siren's call it had been upstairs, but it was still there, lingering in the periphery like a ghost.

Sam wiped her sweaty palms on her skirt and hoped he didn't notice, but Spiros was occupied with checking for traffic and easing out onto the lane.

Snow glittered in the glow of the streetlights, and with no one else on the road, the entire world felt asleep. Those with common sense had checked the weather and stayed home, while the foolish braved the elements with dubious company.

Spiros remained as taciturn as ever, his gloved hands firmly on the wheel as his gaze never wavered from the road. His driving was careful and unhurried, and at this speed, it would be an even longer drive if they had to spend it in silence.

Surprisingly, he broke the quiet first. "Ash."

"What?"

"You keep calling me Spiros. Ash is fine."

Sam opened her mouth, then closed it. Small talk? Not where she thought this would go, or that they would have a conversation at all. Maybe he didn't want the silence any more than she did, especially when it felt so heavy. As if all the unspoken things grew larger the less they said.

"Okay, Ash," she finally said, trying out his name on her tongue. It felt softer, more intimate than Spiros. She wasn't sure that was a good thing. "I have a question."

So many, many questions. He had no idea.

"Yes?"

*Keep it simple, Sam. Easy and safe.*

"When you..." She fumbled for the words, "disguise yourself, is it something you learned or is it something you knew?"

He didn't answer for a moment, but the quiet felt thoughtful rather than fraught with tension. Likewise, the heaviness in the air seemed to have eased.

"I was taught. Most demons have a way to hide themselves, and for incubi, they blend in using an aspect."

"An *aspect?*"

"That's what my handlers called it."

"Your...handlers."

Sam trailed off. This felt like one of those unsafe areas to prod, where her curiosity might lead to him clamming up. She decided to try anyway. How could she know her boundaries if she didn't test them?

"Handlers as in, you were some kind of soldier? Or agent?"

His smile was quick, a baring of teeth. "Not quite."

Sam kept her focus forward, watching the heavy snowfall flicker before the headlights. It was easier than looking at his face and the bitter expression there.

"An aspect is just another term for a demon's mode of disguise," Ash said. "I blend in, though that's the nice term for it. Infiltrate is more accurate."

*A bee from an enemy colony,* Sam thought, moving amongst the workers undisturbed, no alarms raised until after the queen is dead.

"So you can feed without causing a panic," she said.

"Correct."

There was too much weight for a single word. Something in her chest ached, and her desire to ask more questions faded. In another lifetime and different set of circumstances, she might have reached across the distance and touched his shoulder.

Sam remained quiet in her seat and imagined herself as small as possible. It wasn't difficult. Ash commanded such a large presence it felt like something she could wrap herself with, get lost in. A thought that was surprisingly comforting rather than smothering.

What should have been a fifteen-minute drive turned into a half-hour crawl. Ash navigated the snow-laden streets that hadn't yet been touched by a snowplow, his driving cautious and sensible.

*More dad than demon,* Sam thought.

She closed her eyes and leaned against the door, cheek resting against her bent arm. The mark under her glove had cooled, satisfied with a duty fulfilled. A duty Sam had no choice but to obey.

Ash called her name so softly she almost missed it, and she sat up with a wince. There was a sore spot on her neck and pins and needles in her hand. It took her brain a moment to catch up. The engine was silent, and the car was parked in front of her building.

The small overhead light cast a yellow pall over the interior of her car. It highlighted the demon's face, though right now, it was easy to forget he wasn't human. The sharp cheekbones, the even slope of his nose, and the deep set of his brow gave him a permanent intensity that he lacked in the old photos she'd found.

He would be nice to look at, if she didn't feel like he was constantly disapproving of her.

"Sorry." Sam's apologized. "Guess I was tired."

The hard lines of his frown smoothed into something gentler. "No need to be sorry."

Ash looked out the windshield, drumming his fingers on the wheel for a moment.

"I haven't found anything concrete yet about the *signum*. Where it came from. Why you have it." His fingers went still and tightened along the curved surface. "I won't stop trying, but I'm sorry I don't have better news. It wasn't supposed to be like this."

Sam wasn't the only one suffering, she realized. Shame tickled down her spine like an unpleasant flow of icy water.

"It's okay." Sam leaned toward him, but he wouldn't meet her eyes. "You didn't want this either. I get that."

He said nothing, and she glanced at his hands still on the wheel, covered in gloves, his mark hidden beneath.

"Isn't there someone we can contact?" she asked, the thought only springing in her mind now. "Go to for help or advice? There must be others who know about demons too, people who might know what's happening to us."

The silence continued for so long that Sam thought he might never break it. He stared straight ahead at the blanket of snow that had built up on her windshield, a soft barrier separating them from the outside world.

"There are those knowledgeable in these things, yes."

Hope filled her heart, blooming like the petals of a flower, but they curled and blackened at his next words.

"But they won't be able to help us."

"Why?"

His jaw flexed, and his nostrils flared. "The reasons don't matter. They aren't a viable option."

Sam's fists dug into her skirt. Awfully presumptuous, wasn't he?

"That's not helpful," she said through her own frown. "If you explain it to me, maybe I'll understand, maybe I won't. Why don't you give me a chance to try?"

He remained quiet.

"You can't protect me from what's happening, Ash. I'm already involved."

"I know that."

He took another breath, and Sam was reminded of a horse snorting and shaking its head at a buzzing fly.

"I know this isn't easy, and I'm not trying to make it harder. At this point, all I can do is not make the situation worse."

*Worse?* How could it possibly be worse than her body having its own internal countdown timer to doomsday, and the only way to reset it was with the most debauched sex imaginable?

Okay, the debauchery probably wasn't necessary, but it somehow always turned out that way. If they could have clinical sex, go through the steps with machine efficiency, maybe it would be easier.

But the way he touched her and held her close was more animal than machine—

Ash got out of the car and cold air blasted the interior space, robbing her of the pocket of warmth until he shut the door again.

Sam exited the car and walked briskly to get out of the freezing wind, though Ash moved as if he wasn't bothered by it. He still had her car keys, which also had her apartment keys, tucked into his jeans pocket, and she had no choice but to tail him.

By the time they made it into her building, her teeth chattered, and her nose and ears had gone numb. The interior was warmed by central heating, but Ash was his own radiating source of heat. She angled toward him and walked close enough so their bodies nearly touched.

Ash sent her a sidelong glance but said nothing. At least he didn't tell her to go away.

When Sam reached the door, he fit her keys into the lock without prompting. It was a familiar gesture, almost intimate, as if this were his own home he was returning to.

He stepped back so she could enter first. Monster was there to greet them both with displeased screaming, but as soon as he caught sight of Ash, he gave a flick of his tail and darted off to the kitchen.

Sam followed after the cat, who according to Ash, was not a cat.

"Is hobgoblin a demonic translation for cat?" she asked as she opened a can of food and plopped it onto a paper plate.

"Nope."

His voice came from somewhere in the living room.

"Hobgoblins are...well, I'm not sure, exactly," he continued from out of sight. "They ward off demons, I know that much."

"Mine must be broken."

"On that, we agree."

After placating the monster with a sacrifice of foul tuna, Sam joined Ash in the living room and found him staring at her bookshelf. There wasn't much there besides a meager collection of sci-fi and fantasy, many of which had traveled with her from back home in Spokane. Tolkien and C. S. Lewis sat next to Michael Crichton and Carl Sagan, with Ursula Le Guin wedged in between. The rest of her collection sat in storage boxes until she could afford a place with a reading room.

But he wasn't looking at those. Ash's attention was on the picture frames filled with photos of Sam, her mom, and her sister, though a few showed a young Sam with her father. He was absent from any photo where she was older than ten.

Ash's face was angled away, and his tail hadn't returned so she couldn't use that as a gauge, but his posture was peculiar. His arms were crossed over his chest with rigid shoulders, his expression inscrutable when he turned to face her.

"Where did you find the beast?"

It took Sam a moment to realize he was talking about the cat and not another family member.

"He found me." Her smile was small but sprang on its own. "A few days after I moved in, he showed up and refused to leave. The building doesn't allow animals, so I just...hid him. Or he hides himself. He's weirdly good at it."

"Sounds right. They have a habit of getting into places they shouldn't, and if they don't want to be found, they won't be."

"That's Monster."

The soft look returned, the one Sam was learning to recognize even if she didn't quite understand it.

"It's good you have him."

"Yeah," she said. "He's like family, you know?"

Ash's expression was unreadable, and Sam winced. Right. In her research, she'd discovered the only family he had left was his elderly sister and her children and grandchildren, none of whom knew him. Thinking of her own younger sister, Sam couldn't imagine what it would be like to never see her again. But she did know what it was like to lose a parent, the chasm it left behind. She didn't know why it was hitting her so hard now, making it difficult to swallow past the lump in her throat.

Maybe it was the onslaught of snow outside. When ice storms hit and the power went out, her parents used to break out the candles and boardgames for her and her sister. They turned something potentially frightening into a night of laughter and play.

What did Ash do for the holidays? Or his birthday? Who did he share those moments with? Did he even have friends, or people who knew what he was?

Unable to find the words to broach such a monumental topic, she let the silence win. Wishing she was brave enough to break it.

"I should get going."

The announcement came suddenly, awkwardly, and he kept his head down as he headed for the door.

"Wait."

He paused mid-stride, as if he had half a mind to leave anyway, but she couldn't let him. Not yet. There was so much to say, but she didn't know where to start. So she started where her thoughts had left off.

"Your family," she said, twisting her hands in front of her. "I read about them. Your parents and sister."

His posture was unmoving and steadfast, rooted like a 200-year-old oak in a storm. "What about them?"

"Do they...know?"

"Know what?"

"What happened to you?"

He clicked his tongue against his teeth, an impatient noise or perhaps a bitter one.

"Of course not."

"So, they never had closure."

"I just answered that."

She'd been right. Her isolation was brand new, but he'd been doing this since his disappearance in 1971. Forty-nine years of being cut off from everyone he knew. Forty-nine years of separation from everything that made him human. No wonder he was prickly and cold at times. Honestly, he could be much worse, and still, it would be understandable.

Sam had one bad night, and it was enough for her to bite the head off her co-worker. She could do better. *Should* do better.

She took a step forward, careful she wouldn't spook him. That's what he reminded her of now, a horse ready to bolt.

"Have you ever thought about reaching out to them?" she asked after another timid step. "Have you tried—"

"Stop."

She did.

He glared at the spot next to her, and his fists tightened at his sides. "Don't do that."

"Do what?" she asked, her words quiet in contrast to his unsteady ones.

His voice sounded like it was about to crack. As if *he* were about to crack.

"Don't act as if this situation is anything other than what it is," he growled. "Or that I'm not exactly what I am."

"And what are you?"

That smile again, the fragile one with too many teeth. "Well, I'm not your friend."

She thought she'd been getting used to his thorns and how to avoid their pricks. But that one hurt.

"You don't have to be an asshole *either*—"

He was on her in the blink of an eye, looming over her in full demonic regalia. She'd forgotten how big he was with those wings tucked against his back. His eyes were so dark she wondered if she could provoke another feeding just by sheer anger.

Her heart thundered, body tense and muscles tightening. She really shouldn't want that, to push him to see what he would do. She had a strong feeling that everything she'd seen so far was Ash holding back, restraining himself, probably for her sake. She should do the smart thing and back down, let him retreat to lick the wounds that she was clearly reopening.

Instead, she kept her feet firmly planted and stared him in the eye, refusing to blink first.

His eyes narrowed at her unspoken refusal to surrender.

"This is survival," Ash eventually said, the words grating like gravel. "Not some fairytale with a happy ending. If something happens, if one of us can't get to the other, that mark will kill you. And trust me, dying is a goddamn unpleasant experience."

Sam didn't answer. Couldn't answer.

"Tell me you understand and that we won't have a repeat performance of tonight," he growled again. "We've had two close calls already. I'm not looking for a third."

She heard the words, but all she could do was look up into his face and wonder what had happened to make him this way. He'd been a high school science teacher, beloved and respected as far as she knew, and now he was something else. She didn't know what—he was a stone wall she couldn't get through. He withheld information, kept her at bay, and talked to her like one of his students rather than a person stuck in a mutually shitty situation.

"I get it," she said, and her voice trembled. God, she hated when it did that. "I *get* it. But I didn't ask for this, Ash. I'm trying to handle this my own way, and if that doesn't meet your expectations, then I don't know what to tell you. I'm doing the best I can."

"I know you are."

The admission hurt more than if he'd brushed her off, as if he knew her best wasn't good enough. But she had no one else. She had no one to turn to. All she had was this man who would only touch her when he was forced to.

"And I know you didn't ask for this," he continued, anger

slowly deflating. His tail curled around his leg as if seeking its own comfort. "But I need to know we're on the same page. That's all."

"We are."

It was a page hard to miss, scribbled with big red letters. *Fuck if required, companionship optional.*

And just like that, her defiance, her willingness to push him for answers, her refusal to back down, vanished. Replaced by exhaustion and a need to collect herself for her own wound-licking. She stepped back and looked away, breaking their stalemate.

"I'm tired," she said, her voice flat and colorless. "Think I'll go to bed. Thank you for driving me home."

He opened his mouth, but Sam walked past him to open the front door, making her intentions unmistakably clear.

She half-expected him to say something anyway, but Ash moved past her into the hallway, the permanent frown on his lips. His glance lingered on her before he departed, and heavy silence remained in his wake.

# CHAPTER TWELVE

# ASH

ASH HADN'T GONE FAR, FINDING HIMSELF ONCE AGAIN lingering before her door. He told himself it was to listen and ensure she hadn't collapsed from exhaustion, not because he wanted to pound on her door and beg for her forgiveness. Forgiveness for being an asshole, just like she'd accused. And most of all, for everything he had done and would yet do to her.

He listened at the door. It wouldn't be the first time someone had fainted from his feeding, but he'd been careful to drain her the barest amount he could get away with. Even then, with the combination of stress and the alcohol on her breath, Ash had worried about her getting home.

Just when he was satisfied she wasn't going to pass out and crack her head open on the kitchen tiles, he felt it. A small trickle at the back of his mind, like an echo or a reflection. He felt sadness, longing, something bereft. A hurt he, himself, had caused.

Ash had never really considered this connection they had. It had been useful in moments of danger when he could sense a demon closing in on her. She was like a goddamn flame to hellish moths, and he never did figure out why. It wasn't just the ones that came through the original portal she'd made. Sometimes there were others, popping up like nasty surprises.

He'd kept her alive so far, but by God, it had been a trial, and now the fucking irony was there was nothing he could do about the latest asshole demon who had wrecked her life. Ash rubbed the back of his neck like he was swatting away an annoying bug, but the feeling still persisted.

He closed his eyes, that echoed ache along the connection finding a twin in his chest. There was a part of him, an annoyingly large part, that wanted to go inside, break yet another lock in the process, and pull her close. Not for a feeding, though his track record with innocent touches was akin to that of a chain smoker quitting after twenty years and swearing all he wanted to do was hold a cigarette, *honest.*

Making her feel less alone seemed like the only decent thing to do, and it was also the one thing he couldn't. Ash knew what she was going through, what it was like to have his own body betray him.

Unfortunately, that bastard was still betraying him. Like an addict who just had his latest hit, he couldn't be trusted around his vice.

He opened his eyes and stared at the faded blue paint of her door, the wood as insurmountable as a titanium vault, and he finally turned away.

The flight was unpleasant, freezing winds buffeting Ash like a wayward kite, cold flakes slapping his face and stinging his eyes. It was like a punishment or, at least, a stern commentary on how he'd handled himself tonight.

His home did little to comfort him. The clock tower held a silent chill, only partially due to the snowstorm outside. No matter how much Ash tried, the damn tower refused to warm up in the winter. Now, with the pale light playing shadow puppets through the windows, it resembled a tomb more than a place for the living—which was apropos, all things considered.

Ash often saw himself as more a ghost than a demon, his existence serving as a poor reminder of the man he'd once been. He'd planned to continue on that way, stepping into the living world as little as possible like the shade he pretended to be.

Easier said than done. Ash was a bastard, but not a heartless one, and that was precisely the problem. Even though Samara was still human and would remain that way, he'd lived a version of what she was going through. The horrific changes, the mind-breaking pain, the confusion and fear, and worst of all, the isolation—he'd experienced them all. He could see that same agony in Samara when she tried to reach out to him, communicate, and connect.

Pushing her away was the best thing for her, but no matter how hard he tried to distance himself, to detach and view the situation through a clinical lens, he kept fucking up. He couldn't stop. He was too selfish to let her go.

Mainly, because he couldn't. So long as he had to feed from her, he was going to be attached. Maybe if he hadn't been watching her for years, it would be different. His promise to look out for her had twisted into something predatory and sinister, corrupted beyond repair.

Ash's life had been forfeited long ago, but Samara still had a future, and he was going to make sure she got to see it.

He sat on his bed and stared out the window in the clock face, the city below him laid out like a winterscape of white and black, flecked with sparkling lights faintly blinking through the drifting snow. The tip of his tail swayed back and forth as it usually did when he was entrenched in a problem, but tonight, his thoughts came up empty.

The world was melancholy and silent, and the clock tower had never felt so cold. Even knowing this was how it had to be, that a hollow life was the kindest he could live, Ash felt more alone than he had in a long, long time.

---

He rubbed his eyes, irritated from the late, or rather, early hour. This wasn't the first time Ash had scoured the Tower's library until dawn. Over the past few weeks, he'd made visits nearly every day, but so far had discovered nothing helpful.

He leaned back in the old, wooden chair and watched dust motes glow in the dusky dawn light filtering in through the stained-glass windows lining the back wall. The desk lamp next to his elbow had been his main source of light, though there was the occasional candle or two placed amongst the tall shelves. The Vates didn't seem concerned with leaving open flames near their precious books. They probably enchanted their tomes with some kind of fireproof magic.

Ash wished he'd found something to explain what was making his demonic tendencies go awry. Halloween night hadn't been a fluke. He'd hoped it had been a one-time fuck-up, but no.

He'd fed, not once, or twice, but *three* goddamn times.

Ash's history was a minefield when it came to his body changing and rebelling against him. So now, any time it did something abnormal or strange, he got nervous. And this went beyond the concoction no longer working.

A hungry demon wasn't picky when it came to prey. In that

way, incubi were no different than *Alpen,* feeding when the opportunity arose.

It was unheard of for a demon to crave one particular person, but the demon part of him wanted her and no one else. Ash had thought maybe he could spare Samara the next time he had to feed by choosing someone else, but each time, he was drawn only to her. Feeding on someone else would be like eating out of the garbage to keep from starving.

Feeding from another poor bastard might solve Ash's problem, but Samara's *signum* would still demand her to be fed. By him and no one else, apparently.

It wasn't a fluke, or a mistake, but a fucking disaster.

Ash rubbed the tiredness from his face. If this pattern held, his next hunger cycle would be in a week and a half. After that, he'd return to his weekly feeding schedule, the one he hadn't had to obey for the past twenty-five years because the Vates had given him an alternative. They were the only people who might have the answers, and they were also the people he couldn't turn to for help.

At least, not directly. The mystical scholars had a treasure trove of knowledge he could borrow, hence why he was in the Tower's archive at such an ungodly hour.

The original Vates who helped him acclimatize to life back on Earth had given him limited access to the archives. Living as a "free" demon was a hell of a lot different than living as a bonded slave, and the Department of Defense hadn't exactly left him with an instruction manual on how to deal with his own body and needs.

Not that the Department of Defense would ever acknowledge they'd once had a rogue branch that tried to create obedient demonic soldiers. That information was buried so deep, he wouldn't be surprised if it no longer existed. Records and logs redacted until they were useless pages filled with black lines, or more likely, thrown into a furnace and burned. They certainly would have destroyed the video tapes, the most damning evidence of all. Ash still remembered the cameras trained on him like silent judges, recording every miserable second of his transformation.

Ash squeezed his eyes shut and opened them again. No, his *creators* weren't any help, but his rescuers would be. The Vates could have locked him away or simply banished him back to the fiery pits of Hell (actually a misnomer; there wasn't much fire in the demon realm, but there was a lot of hot sand). Instead, they'd risked their own safety to bring him back from the wild creature he'd become.

Not seeking their aid felt dishonest, but he didn't have a better option. He needed to get a handle on this thing before taking it to a kid who was still far too young to be a leader.

But Ash was running out of ideas. There must be a connection between his returned appetite and Samara's mark, but the archives didn't contain anything about demonic *signums* appearing on humans. All he had to go on was his sudden and inexplicable hunger and the appearance of the mark—a mirrored image of his own— the next morning.

Ash closed the tome he was reading and pushed it aside. He'd seen Samara two days prior and that side of him didn't yet hunger. But his thoughts strayed to her, and not just in the context of the colossal problem he was trying to solve. He kept thinking about the sex.

It was as if an addict who'd been sober for decades had gotten a taste, and proceeded to not just fall off the wagon, but take the reins and drive it off a cliff for good measure.

He'd felt her need at the party and couldn't stay away once

he'd caught her scent, a damn foxhound frenzied in the chase. The feeding hadn't merely taken care of his demonic needs, he'd enjoyed it. To touch her, feel wanted and desired—it was a need he hadn't expected. Probably because it was human.

He tapped the hardwood desk with a nail. Which came first, her mark or his hunger? Everything had been normal until he'd tried to wipe her memory. That had to be the catalyst.

Too bad Ash had no idea what the hell it meant. He'd wiped plenty of minds, passively through feeding and actively through his abilities, and none of them had failed, let alone left a demonic stamp behind.

There was one book that might have the answers, though he didn't have the clearance level for that. Apparently, no one did.

When Ash had asked about it, the Eterna had said in that airy, smooth voice of hers, "keep your thoughts forward-facing and look to what is ahead, rather than what lay behind."

She'd been good at wise-sounding deflection so sturdy you could bounce a bullet off it. But behind everything she said, whether it made sense or not, had been raw wisdom and sage advice. Advice he could use now.

Not for the first time, he wished the Eterna was still alive. He missed her calming presence, her faint smile when she found something amusing, and the way she seemed to have an answer for everything, even if she didn't answer anything with a straightforward remark. She would know exactly what to do in this situation. Ash would have gone to her and told her everything that first night, no question.

But she wasn't here, and that left Ash with only one other repository of knowledge: the *Necronomicon.*

His tail twitched as he planned his best approach. Who was more likely to grant him permission to read an unreadable book?

The stern matron who could probably kill with a stare or the peach-faced boy who should have been left in the Petri dish to grow for a few more years?

Ash stood and stretched his cramped muscles, his wings curling and flexing as his tail arched. It felt damn good to drop his aspect outside of his home. He used to maintain it when he visited the Tower, but that shyness had vanished over the years. They knew he was a monster, could apparently *see* it under his skin, so what was the point in pretending?

So when Ash tilted his head, listened for the sound of footsteps, and found none, he set off for the interior of the Tower. He might not know exactly where the *Necronomicon* was kept, but there were certain parts of the building that contained anti-demonic glyphs etched into the arches, thresholds he couldn't cross. He figured that was as good a start as any.

The vaulted hallways were lit with golden lamps that filled the space with a reverent glow, and it was so silent Ash could hear the soft padding of his shoes on the thick, ornate carpet runners.

Ash wouldn't be able to sense the hidden glyphs until he got close. Passing near one of the protective symbols caused his body to react in strange ways: a tightening of the skin, tension on the nape of his neck, and every hair on his body electrified, not unlike standing under (or flying over) a transmission tower.

Ash sensed a glyph ahead. The demon part of him balked and wanted to flee with his tail tucked between his legs, but instead, he stalked toward the source and walked directly into Norbu.

Ash took a step back. He hadn't seen the Vate come out of the doorway to the right, hadn't even heard her footsteps approaching.

Norbu didn't blink. "I believe the Inumerator gave you perusal of the archives only."

Ash wet his lips. Once upon a time, he was a decent poker player and still would have been if not for his damned tail. The twitchy thing telegraphed too much, unless he forced it still, which he did now. Better for her to suspect he was hiding something than for the truth of it to be as plain as day.

"He did," Ash responded. "Unfortunately, I couldn't find what I was looking for."

"And where do you expect to find answers, if not the archives?"

She was perfectly even, nearly serene, a master of the craft of delivering a loaded question with flawless accuracy.

"Honestly? Not sure." The lie came out smoothly despite his nerves, but a thought occurred to him. Stupid, maybe, but why the hell not? It wasn't as if he had any other resources to turn to. "Actually, I'm glad you're here. Maybe you could help me."

She arched an elegant brow. "Is that so? And what could I possibly help you with?"

*Well, shit. Okay, all right, start small. Fish in the pond before heading for the ocean.*

"What do you know about...hobgoblins?"

"Hobgoblins?"

The increasing slope of her brow transported Ash back to grade school where his homeroom teacher, Ms. Perkins, would give him the glare of doom when he acted out in class—which had been often.

"I came across one while banishing an *Alp.*"

Norbu frowned. "*Alpen* are rare, but mostly harmless. Why did you seek out this one?"

"It came through the portal with me."

"Ah." Understanding smoothed the sharp lines around her

eyes. "It has been some time since you tracked down a fellow traveler, is it not?"

*Fellow traveler,* what a nice thing to call a demon invading a dimensional rift in order to taint the world on the other side.

"Two years," he said.

Ash had found fewer of them over time. Only a handful remained. The others had been hunted down by Ash, the Vates, or a combination of the two. It had been easy to find them in the early years when they used to circle the girl like sharks. Ash didn't know if the demons understood Samara had been the one to release them, or if they simply liked to torment children, because the older she got, the more they lost interest, scattering to the wind.

"And I didn't hunt it down," Ash added. "This one snuck under the radar until it fed on a human, and I sensed it."

Mostly truth.

"That's where I came across the hobgoblin. It, uh...was agitated with the *Alp.*"

"I imagine it would be," Norbu said. "They sense the wrongness of demonic existence and tend to react as a sort of rudimentary alarm system."

At least Ash had been somewhat right about that, though it still didn't explain why the beast tolerated him.

"If, say, there was a hobgoblin in the area, does it mean anything?" Ash was on thin ice. There was information on hobgoblins in the archives, but if Norbu pointed that out, he could always say he was hoping for insight from a more experienced, worldly source.

As if flattery and charm would work. The woman could chew him up and spit him out on an off day.

She pressed her lips together in thought, and Ash took that as a promising sign she wouldn't call out his bullshit.

"They tend to gravitate to locations of dark energy."

*Shit.*

"Are they dangerous?" he asked. Ash really didn't want to be the one to tell Samara she had to get rid of her beast.

"Not necessarily. If you view the energy of the universe as an ecosystem always in flux on a cosmic scale, then the hobgoblins are the...hmm, fungus? I am unsure of their equivalent in a living system. They are drawn to sites of imbalance, such as areas saturated in dark energy, and encourage it to heal."

So, they were detritus feeders. They consumed rot and expelled beneficial molecules back into the ecosystem, such as carbon and nitrogen, or whatever the magical counterpart in this case.

All right, Samara could keep the damn thing.

"Thanks. That's good to know."

Norbu studied him with renewed focus. "Was there anything else?"

*Surely, you didn't spend weeks being stumped by that*, was what he actually heard. She really could give Ms. Perkins a run for her money.

Ash chewed his lip. Could he ask the next question without drawing suspicion? The Vate might connect the dots. She knew of Samara in a roundabout way, and the Vates were nothing if not thorough in their research. Philosophers, scholars, and scientists of a sort, Samara had been the center of their attention briefly, though she wouldn't remember it.

They'd determined the portal was a spontaneous event, and Samara had either been very lucky or very unfortunate, depending on the perspective. The study had been closed, and by now, forgotten.

No one knew Ash had kept tabs. It shouldn't lead back to her, no matter how dubious his inquiries were.

"Yeah, one other thing," he said. "Is it possible for a human... to have a demonic *signum*?"

Norbu stiffened. It was so subtle, so imperceptible, no one but a demon would have sensed it. "Where did you hear such a thing?"

He feigned a shrug, the rest of his attention on keeping his tail locked in place.

"Came across it in one of the books, but there wasn't much detail. I was hoping..." He acted the hell out of the next part with the same gusto he'd given his mom when he pretended to be sick with the flu in sixth grade. Ash let his eyes stray to the wall, which was constructed of old woodwork in this part of the Tower. "... that maybe it meant I could be human again."

The shift in her expression told him something he hadn't known before. A demon could successfully lie to a Vate.

"No," she said. "It's impossible to return to what you once were after the ritual is complete. I'm sorry, Spiros."

Her sympathy was an uncomfortable sting under Ash's skin. He had wanted his humanity returned a long time ago, but he knew hoping for that was as pointless as a fish wishing it had legs.

"I figured," Ash said, not having to fake the disappointment in his voice. "Thought I would ask, anyway."

Norbu was quiet, her expression creased in concentration. "There are a few instances of humans possessing a demonic *signum* on their bodies. If you should come across such an individual, you would do well to create immediate distance. Better yet, inform us so we may handle the situation with the appropriate measures."

"What?" The air was suddenly gone from his lungs, leaving his words without strength. "What does that mean?"

"It means that you have come across an individual who is, for all intents and purposes, no longer beholden to themselves. They belong to a demon."

The sound of static filled his ears, and his body froze like a trapped animal.

Norbu continued to speak, her face grave. "It is not unlike the ownership you once experienced at the hands of your tormentors. Except in this case, the demon is the master, and the human is the slave."

Ash didn't speak. He didn't even breathe.

"And my warning to keep your distance is not to be taken lightly," she continued. "Once in the presence of another demon, the *signum* will activate and alert the demonic master that another encroaches on their territory. After all, this human is not only their possession, but their exclusive food source. These demon masters can still feed from others, certainly, but they prefer to feed from their human. The energy is purer, more potent. Some have described it as an addictive euphoria."

Her frown deepened into a contemplative slant. "It is little wonder you found nothing in the archives. Knowledge of demon pacts is a well-guarded secret. Or rather, a poorly kept one, if you look to popular media for inspiration."

Norbu shook her head in dismissal of what she often called the "unfathomable delight of ignorant children for what they do not understand." Get her started on the mass marketability of Hallow's Eve, and she would go on a rant that would put all of Ash's college professors to shame in terms of passion and length.

Though when pressed, Norbu once admitted there were a handful of horror films she proclaimed as "not entirely insufferable."

"I thought..." He fought to keep down the contents of his stomach. "Demon pacts were a one-way street. That they were the only way for a human to control a demon."

"The true nature of these pacts are poorly understood outside of rare occultist texts." Norbu paused and fixed Ash with another stare that felt like she could wrench the information out of him like a dentist pulling teeth if she only looked long enough. "Have you located such a person during your hunts?"

"An occultist?"

"Don't be cute."

"No, I haven't." His response was automatic even as his mind reeled like a skiff in a storm. "I didn't know it was even possible."

Of course he didn't know. If he did, Ash would never have gone into Samara's apartment, *Alp* be damned. Goddamn leech had been more trouble than it was worth, and Ash wished he could summon it himself so he could kill it again.

"Some of our historic scholars believed a human can only become a slave if they enter into an agreement with a demon, and then break their side of the pact," Norbu said, rubbing the point of her finger against her chin. "Others say the human offers themselves to the demon in exchange for a wish or a gift. The stories vary depending on region and era, but all have a single point on which they agree. The human will bear a mark, one that is specific to their master, and it is burned into their flesh. A branding."

*No.*

"Of course, bound demons cannot enter such a contract."

Her tone clearly indicated the conversation was a purely

academic one, not realizing what was theoretical to her was quickly becoming Ash's worst nightmare. Nor did she seem aware he was having a quiet, internal crisis right in front of her.

"Bound demons cannot possess human slaves, because they themselves are a slave. These pacts can only be created by free, unbound demons—Spiros? Is something wrong?"

Apparently, she'd noticed.

Ash shook his head, a denial rather than an answer to her question.

"I don't understand," he said when he managed to unstick his tongue. "I've never heard of this. General Vogel didn't mention it. Nor did Doctor Tamfield."

The woman's features crinkled in distaste at the mention of those names. "A demon master, particularly one with multiple human slaves, holds great power, far more than a single demon alone. I imagine it's not something your captors would have wanted you to know."

Ash appreciated her use of the word *captors* rather than *masters.* Perhaps not as accurate, but still, appreciated.

There was still one spark of hope he could reach for, with the desperation of a climber hanging on by his fingertips.

"Forming a pact has to be complicated, right? I mean, it's not as simple as a handshake. There's probably blood magic and alchemical ingredients and incantations involved. I'm not looking to make a pact," he added quickly, "I just want to make sure I never..."

His words fell silent, mostly because Norbu looked at him as if he was being particularly stupid.

"No," she agreed. "You cannot accidentally form a bond with a human. Demon pacts take a consensual agreement on both sides. No blood is needed; that is simply conjecture twisted over the millennia."

He didn't want to ask. He didn't. Couldn't he just take that answer and be comforted in knowing he'd never done such a thing?

Apparently not.

"If there's no blood involved, then how does it work?"

Her bright-eyed look was far too excited for the situation, but even she fell into the trap all Vates did when it came to scholarly discussions.

"Historically, blood has been used as a cheap substitute for *animus.* You understand the language, so you know *animus* can mean many things in Latin. The soul, the mind, the heart. It is a person's specific essence. Blood is symbolic for life, and more intimately, as a symbol of sacrifice. To give one's heart to another without literally doing so, an *animus* can truly be anything. Blood was simply the answer for the unimaginative."

Ash's spine stiffened with each word. He wanted to tell Norbu to stop, to not say another word before he heard too much.

His desire for mercy was not granted.

"To finalize the pact," she concluded, "the human must give to the demon something precious and treasured. A true symbolic gesture of giving the demon their heart."

He no longer saw the rich halls of oak and crimson tapestries. Ash stood in a little girl's bedroom covered in sky blue wallpaper, with posters of dinosaurs and stars, a peach-colored bed in one corner, and a small writing desk in another. The owner of the bedroom, so young but unafraid, held something out to him.

*The toy! The goddamn* toy*!*

The world fell away from him, as if he'd waited on the gallows for longer than he could remember, the noose coiled around his neck like an insatiable serpent, and someone had finally dropped the trapdoor under his feet.

"Does that answer your question?"

"Yes," he said, his voice calm, even, and entirely unlike himself. "It does."

The sorcerer nodded, though her gaze on him was watchful. Not that such a look was any different than usual.

"Remember what I said—"

As if Ash could ever forget.

"—if you come across such a person, alert the Inumerator or myself as quickly as you can. A human within the throes of a pact is completely at the demon's mercy, and such a bond often leaves destruction in its wake."

Ash needed to leave. He was hanging on by a thread, and if he broke now in front of the Vate, it was over.

"Right. I'll remember."

He said some kind of goodbye to Norbu and thanked her for the information, but it was distant and strained. He found the nearest stairwell that would take him to the rooftop access, or at least, he hoped it would. The Tower had a way of swallowing you up and spitting you out in a random location if you let your mind wander.

His thoughts didn't wander, they were lost, and his body carried him along each heavy step.

Ash hadn't fucked up two months ago. He'd fucked up twenty-five *years* ago.

*I did this to her. No one else. Not the doctor, or the General, or another demon.*

*Me.*

Ash came to a stop, his world once again tilting as he balanced on the cut stone steps. He braced himself on the rough wall, thankful it was a spiral staircase wrapped inside a circular, stone column.

A string tugged at his chest, the one that tied him to Samara in a way he didn't understand but was beginning to. It only gave a yank when she was in trouble, but this was more like a constant pull, as if she wanted to knock him off his feet and drag him along.

The feeling eventually faded, leaving Ash gasping for breath as he clutched the front of his shirt. Left in its wake was an empty feeling, a hollow pit ringed with a forlorn ache.

For one damning minute, he feared she was dead. God knew she was skilled at getting into trouble, but even she had the sense to avoid extreme danger. No, she wasn't dead. He could still sense her, though at a great distance, the gulf between them growing wider by the second and at a great speed.

There was only one thing that could draw her away so quickly and without warning.

"Son of *a bitch.*"

He bolted up the staircase, stripping his jacket as he went. It looked like he wouldn't be going home anytime soon.

## CHAPTER THIRTEEN

# SAM

*The girl walked through the forest though she didn't know where she was going. The path was ill-trod, covered in damp undergrowth which held the moisture of recent rainfall.*

*It always rained here, a perpetual drizzle that paused to the held breath of the air.*

*Quiet. No birdsong, no buzzing or skittering of insects, and the only disturbance to the foliage was a constant drip-drip-drip. Humidity clung to her skin like plastic wrapped around leftovers, and the girl couldn't remember why she was here.*

*One bird was brave enough to sing, followed by another, until the canopy once again filled with life, as if mocking the next storm that darkened the horizon.*

*The girl stopped, but the birds continued to sing. A man stood on the path behind her, his face a shadow within the hood of his jacket. Water dripped from the waterproof material—the only movement that touched him.*

*The man spoke. "You shouldn't be alone."*

*She said, "I'm not alone," because that was the truth. He was here.*

*Nothing had changed about the man, but she knew her words angered him.*

*"Go back to your mother."*

*The voice was a growl. She recalled tales of grizzlies preying on lost hikers in the woods.*

*"Why?"*

*When he took a step forward, the girl took a step back. Again came the thought of grizzlies and other things in the dark, though she couldn't imagine what was scarier than a hungry bear.*

*"Go. Back."*

*Another step in retreat. Another. The girl wasn't afraid, but she wasn't stupid. Her family's campsite wasn't far, but it wasn't close enough for someone to hear her screams.*

*"I'm not lost," she told the man. "And I'm fine on my own."*

*Another step. Her heel caught on a vine, but she pulled free of the tangle.*

*"Leave. Now."*

*His sharp tone cut through her, and she was no longer a girl unafraid. She turned to run. She could easily lose the man in the twisting trails and wild undergrowth, but her chance was snatched away.*

*On the path before her, a massive bear rose onto its hind legs, its matted brown fur dark and oozing with worms that writhed and crawled. Pale bone peeked through the places where meat and fur rotted away, and its skull stared down at her, its eye sockets empty.*

*But through the emptiness of where its eyes should be, it could see her.*

*The girl froze, and cold seeped through her bones as the darkness spread through the trees. The rain returned in dreary sheets, and as it soaked her, the girl imagined it became frost on her skin.*

*The bear opened its rotted maw wide, sinew anchored muscle to bone in an anatomical display. Its roar shook the trees, and the birds took flight, the insects went silent, and the darkness encroached, making itself at home in the nooks and hollows.*

*The bear raised a dripping paw, the width of a car tire, and the girl didn't move. Not out of stubbornness or a child's refusal to listen. She simply couldn't.*

*With a tight grip on her shoulder, the man flung her backwards, shoving her behind him. The girl lost her footing, and as she fell, the bear brought down its paw on the man's head.*

Sam opened her eyes.

Snowflakes battered the round window, and she saw they hadn't left the tarmac. The plane had been delayed by an hour, and they'd had to wait an hour more onboard until conditions improved.

With how tired she still was after the party, falling asleep wasn't surprising. The old dream was, though. She hadn't had it in a long time.

She watched the technicians finish spraying the airplane wings with a chemical to make sure ice wouldn't stick to the metal, negating lift and dragging them down into a spiral of death.

Sam wondered if Ash ever had problems flying in the cold, if the leathery flaps of his wings were prone to freezing. It was still hard to believe those wings could even get him off the ground, but after all the things she'd experienced in the last two months, flying should seem routine by now.

It wasn't, and knots twisted her stomach as the plane got moving again, taxiing onto the long stretch of runway that would give it space to take off. The engines began their slow roar, like a racecar revving up before taking off at the starting line.

Sam thought it was more akin to climbing a very long ascent on a roller coaster and then perching on the peak, waiting for the drop. Her insides churned, anxiety and anticipation mingling into a confusing mess of exhilaration and fear.

It was a feeling Sam was coming to find familiar, and as the airplane rocketed down the runway, it wasn't unlike when she was within a demon's grasp, helpless and out of control.

And then the front of the plane lifted, followed by the back wheels, and that feeling of heavier gravity clenched her body in a breathtaking vise. The passengers around her simply waited, quiet and bored. Sitting inside a metal tube rocketing through the air had become so commonplace that it was now mundane.

One could become used to anything, she supposed.

The plane climbed smoothly to cruising altitude, and Sam's fellow passengers relaxed and pulled out phones or tablets or books. A couple of them wandered from their seats and a few unbuckled their belts.

Sam kept hers firmly in place.

Not for the first time, she wondered if this was safe. The trip had been spontaneous, a flash of inspiration that forced her to send a flurry of emails. Only three sent a reply, with two of them having to decline her inquiry due to the fact they no longer lived in the area.

But the last email she received had her buying a roundtrip ticket to Phoenix, Arizona.

Sam had visited a few of the hot spots along the West Coast. Anaheim for several family trips to Disneyland, Las Vegas with a couple of college friends, and a drive along the Alcan Highway with her sister after Sam earned her bachelor's degree.

She'd never been to Arizona before, and she wouldn't be staying in Phoenix for long. The sun-scorched city was only the first stop on her trip.

"First time flying?"

Sam glanced at the woman sitting next to her. Old enough to be Sam's mother, or perhaps an older aunt, she had a friendly face behind her round glasses, her hair frozen in dark curls.

"No," Sam said, sounding exactly as if it was. "I've flown before."

"First time alone, then?"

Sam supposed it was. She nodded, and the woman gave a sympathetic tsk of her teeth.

"Nothin' to it. I'm going to see my granddaughter in Mesa. Are you visiting family?"

Sam tried to keep up with the unidentifiable accent she could only describe as *country*.

"Uh, not exactly. It's a research assignment."

"That right? You some kind of academic?"

"No, nothing like that." Sam gave a little rueful smile. "More like an amateur journalist."

"Oh, that's lovely." The woman leaned in with a conspiratorial tilt. "Lots to do and see in the Valley. You're visiting at a good time of year too. Every day is beautiful and just the right temperature."

"That's what I've heard," Sam lied. She didn't know a damn thing about where she was going, an error in hindsight. She'd been too eager to catch her taxi for the airport, stuffing random bits of winter clothes into her bag.

"You should find something to keep you occupied," she said, pulling out a book of crossword puzzles and giving Sam a squinty smile. "Makes the time go by faster."

"Good advice."

The woman smiled again before diving into her book of puzzles, and Sam took a slow full breath when it felt safe to do so. The woman hadn't introduced herself by name, and Sam knew more about her than she did most of her neighbors. She wasn't sure if that said more about the woman or Sam.

Her seat was too stifling and uncomfortable for another nap, so she pulled out her phone. Her laptop was in her bag somewhere above her head, and she almost regretted not having it. It was going to be a long three hours.

She spent the time going over the articles she'd stored in her phone, marking down notes and questions she wanted to ask. She hadn't been lying when she claimed to be an amateur journalist. That was the route she was going with in her email as well. She had given the impression she researched cold cases as a "personal interest." It felt more tactful than saying she enjoyed digging up missing person cases as a hobby. Less creepy, too.

By the time the seatbelt light flashed on and the captain announced their beginning descent, Sam felt like she had a handle on what she was doing. Her gut still churned with nerves, but there was a set to her spine that was typically absent.

She was finally doing something. Whether or not she knew where it would lead was a different matter, but goddamn if she wasn't doing it.

The turbulence was rocky enough for Sam to clutch the edges of her seat, but the woman (Grace, she'd finally learned) patted her hand and said, "This is nothing. Try landing in the summer with those heat waves comin' off the city!"

Sam didn't take a full breath until the wheels touched down, smooth as gliding on ice. She didn't know how people could take these harrowing journeys and go about their day when all that had separated them from death was a thin layer of metal and carbon composite.

She bid Grace goodbye after the crowded shuffle to get off the plane, and with her bag in hand, Sam followed the crowd out of the terminal. The main hub of Sky Harbor contained a plethora of bars, food joints, and gift shops containing an overabundance of cactus themes. Sam had never seen a saguaro in person before, but she doubted they stuck out their green arms at such cartoonish angles.

After waiting in an impatient, edgy line at one of the car rental counters, Sam signed the forms and had a pair of car keys clutched in her hand. She had to shield her eyes from the intrusive glare of sunlight determined to blind her while she located her rental in the lot.

Grace's comment about the bright sunshine was like saying it got cold in Alaska. Obvious, but understated.

The inside of the silver sedan was uncomfortably warm, as if it was August in Seattle rather than December in Phoenix. She was already sweltering in her long-sleeved shirt, her jacket long abandoned on the passenger seat as she cranked up the AC.

The car came with a GPS screen, a luxury Sam could get used to, and she white-knuckled her way out of the desert capital, heading east on the 202. She got out of the city just before rush hour hit, escaping the traffic congestion without a second look back.

Saguaros, it turned out, did look cartoonishly goofy with their barrel arms raised toward the sky like the loser in an old Western duel. Sam only stopped once at a gas station to grab some snacks for the road, the sunset at her back painting a hue of colors across the sky, smeared orange and fire yellow with purple dusk at the edges.

What struck her was the starkness of the hills, how bare and exposed they were below a sky that seemed impossibly big. Sam breathed easier once trees began to appear, sparse at first, then thick with dry, piney trunks and branches. She'd passed a few signs of life along the two-lane highway, small towns with big names like Superior and Globe, still surrounded by desert scruff.

But once she entered the forests, the darkness took on a suffocating feel, smothering any lights except those of other vehicles. Signs announced she had entered the Fort Apache Reservation, but she couldn't see much beyond the headlights.

Show Low was a strange blend of pine forest and prairie hills. For a moment, she thought she was back home, approaching Spokane from the west just outside of Cheney, stretches of dry meadow and ponderosas mixing together in an iconic blend of what was known as the wild frontier.

And then Sam's vision settled into place as she passed a local theatre, its unfamiliar name fixing her in the correct coordinates. She was a good thousand miles from home, the constant need to pop her ears confirming she was far from the lowlands of eastern Washington.

The last thing she expected to see flashed white between the trees, caught in the headlights with a furtive glow. More of it appeared on the banks next to the highway, pristine and soft.

Sam had crossed the country from the Puget Sound to the Sonoran Desert, and still, she couldn't get away from the snow. To her credit, she hadn't really thought about snow in Arizona, but at least she would be in familiar settings.

A new sign announced she was entering the Apache-Sitgreaves National Forest, close to her journey's end. A half hour later, she turned onto the road that ran through central Aspen Falls, a town whose population had grown but still couldn't surpass the 5,000-occupancy mark.

It was after nine and most of the town stores seemed to be shutting down for the night. Curio shops, hat and shoe stores, bars and gun shops pressed up against each other as if huddling for warmth. She kept her car along the main street until she came to a turnout down a thinly paved road.

Cedar Park Resort wasn't like any resort she had ever seen. The woman at the front desk eyed her with a wary curiosity that made Sam want to shrink, but she held her ground. After listening to a long list of rules (no parties, no drinking, no roughhousing or destruction of property), Sam handed over payment and received a set of keys on a green, diamond-shaped fob with the resort's name etched into the plastic.

Back in her car, Sam drove a little deeper into the property. The rooms weren't rooms so much as they were shared prefab buildings split in half. She was reminded of military housing, or construction site offices, but once she parked her car and went inside, she was relieved to find her room was clean and tidy. It was also quite cozy, with pine furniture, including the bed frame.

Not bothering to take off more than her shoes, Sam crawled into bed and fell into a stupor only the travel-weary could achieve.

---

The morning greeted her with aches and pains. Her backside and legs were sore, reminding her she was halfway through her thirties. Signs of aging had begun creeping up on her in her late twenties, but they were still surprising...and annoying.

Grimy and in need of a muscle relaxant, Sam found the shower worked, though the pressure and hot water didn't feel like they would last long, so she didn't linger.

After sending out an email to confirm she was in town and that she would meet her contact soon, Sam grabbed some food at the local breakfast place, which doubled as a bar and looked like it had once been a saloon. The smell of fresh, robust coffee greeted her as she grabbed a place at the bar, trying to be courteous of the fact she was a single party. She'd been worried everything might be closed on a Sunday, but it was a full house.

Waiting for her order, Sam gazed around the saloon-turned-breakfast pub and admired the various trinkets nailed to the walls. There were horseshoes, black-and-white photos, and more than one pair of antlers, but thankfully no mounted heads stared down at her mournfully.

She wondered if Ash had come here. He must have been to most places in town, at least the ones that existed in 1971, which would be most of them if Sam had to take a guess. What did a high school science teacher do for fun out in the boondocks? Probably anything he could, and she bet he'd visited that bar more than once.

There was one thing she knew for certain—the incubus would not appreciate her prowling his old stomping grounds. Which was exactly why she hadn't asked permission to leave the city over the weekend. It was her business, not his, and she would catch a red eye flight out of Phoenix tomorrow at midnight, just in time for a couple hours of sleep before work.

He probably wouldn't even know she was gone.

Sam dug through her pancakes, hash browns, and orange juice at a steady pace. She had time to explore before her noon appointment, and wanting to stretch her legs after the long drive, Sam walked the main road which appeared to be the tourist trap part of the town with local gifts and souvenirs aimed at travelers. She meandered in and out of the shops, keeping warm with her jacket tucked around her and walking at a brisk pace between stops. It was a fun glimpse into small-town life in the mountains, but ultimately unhelpful. If she wanted to learn more about Ash's previous life, she wouldn't find it in giftshops.

One place caught her eye as she headed back to her car. Potted plants and glittering beads on threads hung in the shop window, and beyond the glass were several aisles of books.

A bell chimed as she opened the door, and the smell of incense warmed her after the chill winter air. Aspen Falls had a familiar aroma. The potent ponderosa pine smell was so much stronger here than it was back home, and the scent of it kept drawing her thoughts to someone she didn't want to think about.

This shop she'd entered had its own personality separate from the town outside. Displays were filled with transparent tubes of colorful beads, thick blankets with angular patterns were folded on a table, leatherbound shoes that looked handmade were set behind a glass case, and dreamcatchers dangled with beads and feathers along a wall. Another table held bundles of sage, various powders, and abalone shells.

The woman behind the counter had purple streaks in her dark hair. From her young age, her various piercings, and the tattoos peeking out from under her sleeves, Sam guessed she was on winter break from college in the city.

"Hey," she said, not looking up from her magazine.

"Hi," Sam replied.

Thankfully, the woman didn't inquire more than that, and Sam was left on her own to peruse the wares. She found a display of crystals and minerals laid out in boxes with their names labeled in attached cards, everything from amethyst geodes to peach-colored quartz to smooth, black opals.

There were plenty of ferns and succulents in pastel-colored pots, but Sam couldn't tell if they were for sale or aesthetic. Bundles of sage smudge sticks lined one shelf, and another wall held ceremonial kachina dolls, their sightless eyes seeming to follow as she passed.

Sam found herself in the book aisle. One drew her attention, and she pulled it out, the green cover rough against her fingers. The cloth reminded her of something, but she wasn't sure what. Old hymnals? There was no title on the front, and when she opened the book, she was disappointed to find the inside pages were blank. It was beautifully bound, and the weight was satisfying and solid in her hands, but she didn't have any use for an empty journal.

Sam lifted the tome to put it back, but her fingers remained firm around the spine. Maybe she could use it. It wasn't as if she didn't have a myriad of confusing experiences to document.

Apparently, it had been decided, because she was standing at the counter and fishing out her wallet from her bag.

The woman eyed the book, then Sam, and said, "Nobody buys those."

"Oh?" Sam said as a placeholder, because she had no idea what to say.

"Yeah. Gran binds them herself."

"They're beautiful."

"Mmm," she hummed, and with a few buttons on the till, she rang out Sam and handed her a printed-out receipt. "See ya."

"Bye."

Sam felt a little windswept, like there was something else she should say but it had flown out of her head. Instead, she slipped the book in her bag, left the shop, and returned to her rental. She entered an address into the GPS—it was close enough to lunch to start for her next destination which was about twenty-minutes away.

She was glad for the rental's GPS; the roads turned to rough concrete at one point, and then eventually dirt, though the driveway she turned onto was a nice, gripping gravel. The house was a beautiful, two-story log cabin with a detached double garage. Pine trees hugged the elevated back porch. Since the cabin was built on a hill, she imagined the view of Bearpaw Lake was gorgeous from up there.

Sam carefully tucked her envy away as she rang the doorbell, and a musical lilt chimed from inside. The door opened a few seconds later, and Sam was greeted by a man in his early sixties. His black and silver hair was pulled back into a long braid.

He extended his hand to shake hers firmly. "Ms. Wandern?"

"That's me," Sam replied, immediately off kilter from his unexpected warmth. "Thanks for agreeing to speak to me, Mr. Kuvaqa."

"My pleasure. Come inside, sit."

Sam followed him, gazing around the home as he shut the door behind her. It was just as lovely on the inside, with warm rugs covering the hardwood floor—real wood, not like Sam's cheap vinyl—and a large Christmas tree situated in the corner between large bay windows. The tree looked like it could have been cut down from just outside—and probably had been.

Sam also noted the tinsel and fairy lights along the mantle and above the windows.

Following her gaze, Mr. Kuvaqa said, "My wife is the big Christmas decorator of the house. She's visiting our youngest in Paradise Valley before they all drive up for the holidays."

She nodded, spotting the family photos laid out on the coffee table, a table that was made of carved petrified wood. On the table was a photo album opened to one page and an old yearbook. Sam's heart leapt in her chest when she saw the yearbook was from 1971.

"Would you like anything? Water? Some juice?"

"No, thank you." She gestured to the yearbook, unable to keep her eyes off it. "May I?"

"Go right ahead."

She perched on the edge of the couch cushion, poised as if ready to take flight, and picked up the book.

As she carefully turned the old pages, Mr. Kuvaqa said, "I was surprised to get your email. It's been a long time since I thought about Mr. Spiros. Not many people care to remember the case."

His question reminded her that she was supposed to be playing a role. She pulled out the voice recorder from her bag and asked, "May I record this?"

"Please do."

Sam placed the recorder on the table and turned it on, and she hovered there, nervous, knowing she should say something professional like her name, or ask him for his, but she was frozen. Emailing this man and pretending to be a cold case, freelance investigator was a lot different than being welcomed into his home and feeling like the shittiest liar.

"Try around page 50 or so," Mr. Kuvaqa said. "The science club should be around there somewhere."

Thankful for the prompt, Sam dutifully flipped to the suggested page, and she skimmed a few of the afterschool clubs. Hunting, fishing, knitting, and camping—the science club stood out among more practical, sensible hobbies.

There was a gaggle of kids, mostly boys but a few girls, their fashion that of the late 1960s. Most of their clothing looked secondhand and as if it had been tended by more than a few sewing needles.

And in the middle of the group, smiling wide, was Ash.

Sam could hardly believe it. This was a much better photo than what she could dig up online, and she saw some of the man she glimpsed in rare, fleeting moments. His smile was bright and charming, nothing like the scowls and frowns he wore now.

"That's him," Sam said, and then cleared her throat as in excuse for the breathless quality.

"I know all kids think this about at least one of their teachers, but he really was the coolest, or at least the best I ever had. If you turn, I think it's the next page, you'll find the art club."

Sam did so, tearing her eyes away from the sepia picture reluctantly. She did find the art club, and there were more girls in this one, their dresses long and floral. A grown woman stood amongst them.

"His fiancée, Ms. Higgens. They were engaged a year before his disappearance, if I remember right. She was kind, sweet—hell, they both were."

Katharine Higgens had been a pretty, slim brunette with pale features tanned by constant sunlight. She had just the kind of face that was made to have a handsome husband. Sam imagined they would have had quite the charmed life if circumstances had allowed it.

"She didn't stick around long after. It kinda shook up the town, not that anyone would admit it."

Sam's head perked up. She chose her response with slow and careful consideration, and although asking these kinds of questions was expected, she still feared she was going to slip up and expose herself as a fake. She was pretty sure pretending to be an investigator could be considered fraud.

"I couldn't find much about the police investigation. But they *did* investigate?"

His disdainful snort was an answer as much as anything else. "Enough to not be accused of negligence, but it was clear they wanted the case closed as soon as possible. Disappearances from the rez were one thing, but a missing teacher from Aspen Falls? That was ugly business."

"Wait. What disappearances?"

Mr. Kuvaqa sighed with a weight that had been invisible until now, and his warm expression was replaced by distant but not forgotten sorrow. "I remember my parents talking about it when they thought I was in bed. Kids going missing. It was just a thing that happened. As I got older, I realized how bad it was, but back then it was almost normal. My cousin was one of the last to disappear, he lived on the Kywu Reservation. That's when Mr. Spiros got involved."

Sam was glad she was recording this; she wouldn't have been able to keep up with the information by hand or laptop.

"Got involved?"

"My parents took me out of school for a little while after my cousin disappeared, and that's how he found out." He paused, his eyes looking past her to see something distant in time rather than physical space. "I told him about the other rez kids that had gone missing, and he got this quiet kind of anger. It was the only time he ever got scary, but I knew he wasn't mad at me."

He rubbed his face and then sent Sam a tired smile. "To be honest, I'm glad you contacted me. Only person I ever told this to is my wife, and it's been a hard thing to carry all these years."

"What?" Sam asked. The yearbook was cradled against her chest, and she didn't remember putting it there. "What is it?"

That tired smile formed into the unmistakable angles of guilt.

"Mr. Spiros is dead because of me."

## CHAPTER FOURTEEN

# SAM

Sam's mind was distant and strangely fragile, the music coming from the car speakers turned down, background noise for her thoughts. The voice recorder had been a smart idea, a last-minute purchase during her scramble to pack for the trip, but she didn't think she would forget that conversation any time soon.

Mr. Kuvaqa, as misplaced as his guilt and self-blame was, had been an open source of knowledge. Sam hadn't dreamed she'd find so much information from this single trip.

The newspaper articles had made it seem that Ash's disappearance had been a one-time phenomenon, a tragic but extraordinary occurrence, like being struck by lightning while safely tucked inside a house.

Ash hadn't been some unlucky bystander. He'd intentionally put himself in harm's way because he thought the authorities weren't looking for those missing kids hard enough.

According to Mr. Kuvaqa's testimony, the reservation police had done what they could with the resources available, but the county deputies had put in a lackluster effort, and they hadn't located any of the children.

And when Ash had gone looking, he, too, had vanished, never to resurface.

Except he had. And he'd been changed beyond recognition.

Sam didn't know how, she didn't understand what had happened to him or who had taken him, but Mr. Kuvaqa had some answers for her there, too.

"It was decommissioned almost fifty years ago, not long after Mr. Spiros went missing," he'd told her, writing a set of directions on a notepad before tearing it off and handing her the paper. "But that place was at the epicenter of the disappearances. Ask around and folks will plead ignorant, but we all remember the strange lights and eerie sounds coming from that part of the valley. If Mr. Spiros went looking for my cousin, that's where he did it."

Aspen Falls High School, closed for the winter break, was a low, squat building constructed of off-white painted brick. It looked almost out of place with the mountainous forest backdrop, especially with the football field next to it, lined on either side with white bleachers. The whole school could have fit with Anytown, USA, except for the fact it looked old. Even a fresh coat of paint couldn't shake the austere, mid-twentieth-century feel of it.

Sam sat in her car in the high school parking lot, the engine still running, as if her decision had already been made. And really, it had been. Whatever was left of Ashley Kane Spiros's life, she wouldn't find it here. She'd already driven past his childhood home, and the small rental he'd been living in during his teaching years.

Those places hadn't provided much of a glimpse into his life, and Sam guessed the same would be said if she visited his old university, Arizona State College, now known as NAU. She didn't have the time or inclination to take a jaunt up to Flagstaff, anyway.

The GPS wouldn't be any help for her next destination. Holding Mr. Kuvaqa's note in one hand, she pulled out of the parking lot. The sun would set within the hour, and she didn't want to be caught out in the dark, not where she was headed.

A few paved lanes and gravel roads later, she crawled past a sign announcing the property beyond belonged to the US government, and all who trespassed would be arrested or face worse consequences. Perhaps even more ominous and effective at keeping out trespassers was a sign warning of ionizing radiation.

The sign was old, rusted through with time and a few potshots taken by bored locals. Sam pushed past it, the gate long gone, with abandoned beer cans and bottles piled around as if mocking the sign's empty threats.

The gravel road gave way to dirt, the twin tire treads long faded with overgrown grass and dislodged rocks threatening her tires and undercarriage. Sam navigated them with the music turned down, as if a lack of volume would help her spot the hazards sooner.

After a few minutes of treacherous navigation, the road opened into a massive field. There were bunkers, watchtowers, barracks, warehouses, and even a rudimentary airstrip at the end of the compound.

She froze, her car slowing to a timid crawl, but there was no sign of life other than a small herd of elk trotting into the woods. A large bird of some kind, a hawk or an eagle, sailed low over the field before disappearing into the trees.

This was stupid. *Really* stupid. Even if no one was around, there were still black bears in the area, along with the rare mountain lion.

She parked her car next to the biggest building she could see, turned off the engine, and left with only her keys and phone. She tucked her bag in the footwell of the passenger side, not too concerned with would-be thieves. There had to be much more interesting things around than her thin wallet and drained bank account.

The fear of her exploration being hampered by locked doors turned out to be unfounded. All of the doors had been removed a long time ago, leaving gaping entrances that led into darkness.

The flashlight on her keychain didn't reach far, and Sam cursed that she hadn't charged her phone last night. She'd fallen right into bed, and now the battery showed a worrying 19%. To her credit, she hadn't planned on trespassing on government property and exploring a decrepit army base.

At least, she assumed it was army, she actually had no idea. She didn't even see a name for the fort, or any kind of signs since the first one she'd blatantly ignored. She was ignoring a lot of things, such as the tiny voice of reason that told her not to go inside the open entrance that looked like a hungry mouth waiting to swallow her.

Sam pulled in her jacket tighter and lifted the scarf over her nose and mouth. It was cold, but it felt different than home. Washington was far enough to the north that the Arctic air crept down and coated everything with a biting frost that wouldn't ease for months.

This kind of chill was caused by elevation and a thinner atmosphere, as if the Earth lacked a firm hold from this height. Even the short walk around the town had her gasping for breath to get the oxygen she needed.

The chill inside was of a third kind, one that spoke of dark places deep in the earth, uninhabited and with a desire to stay that way. She took a few steps through the doorway, and the immediate drop in temperature almost made her back out, but she continued on, her flashlight guiding her path. Debris and rot littered the tile floor, some of it from parts of the ceiling sagged inward, and others she didn't want to think about.

She seemed to be in some kind of staging area, and she kept going forward. It was shockingly dark even without doors, and she realized none of the rooms held windows.

She couldn't imagine what it would have been like fifty years ago. She couldn't imagine Ash here, either. Had he been dragged down these halls, taken into custody after having been caught on the property line?

Mr. Kuvaqa seemed to believe that was the case, but Sam didn't know how that could lead to Ash's disappearance and eventual demonification. The two were most likely unrelated, and whatever had happened to Ash and the children probably had nothing to do with what seemed to be a standard military fort.

And yet, she was here, because she knew the chance of them being unrelated wasn't zero.

There wasn't much on this level except dusty rooms and abandoned offices full of random furniture and empty filing cabinets. To explore further, Sam would have to descend, and the open maw of the elevator shaft gave her such a visceral reaction of dread that she gave it a wide berth.

She found a metal staircase that seemed stable enough; it didn't shake or tremble under her, just a faint creak every few steps. Sam could only hope that didn't mean there was a severe case of metal fatigue. She supposed she would find out soon enough, and with her phone showing no access to any cell tower, it would be a long time before anyone found her.

*Stupid,* she repeated. Really *stupid*.

The next level down appeared to be more offices, so she kept going further and further, each floor becoming more decrepit and littered with detritus. Sam kept the scarf over her nose, wishing for even the barest mask as rank and festering scents battered her senses. Black mold and asbestos exposure hadn't been on her itinerary.

At least all the doors on the first floor were open and she didn't have to worry about running out of air or being trapped inside. A small comfort, one that did little as the darkness followed on her heels, the kind that hadn't seen light in so long it might as well be another world, buried and forgotten.

The last floor was where she stopped, six if she was counting correctly. This one was different. A massive double door barred her way, with clear windows on either side of it.

The first thing that came to mind was a vault. One window was entirely coated by dust on the inside, and the other was clouded but not completely opaque. Sam cleaned it with the sleeve of her jacket and looked inside, holding the flashlight at chest height.

Sam's fingers twitched violently, and the light flashed along the wall and floor as she fumbled it. She brought it back up to the window, the light shaking in her unsteady grip, her breath fogging the glass. It was almost like a mercy, trying to block her sight from what was inside.

Cages. Rows and rows of them lining the wall, their bars in crisscrossing black wires, like dog crates. Some of them small, but most of them large enough to fit a grown man.

The stairs creaked behind her. Sam spun so fast her shoulder hit the wall, and she lowered her flashlight again, choking down a scream as she brought it up a second time.

Ash blinked at the light in his face and shielded his eyes with his hand, but it didn't block his expression or the whipping snap of his tail.

"Ash." Her words were gasping, panicked things, torn between relief, fear, and most of all, embarrassment. "What the *fuck*—what are you *doing* here?"

"Are you seriously asking me that right now?"

He took a step forward. Sam scrambled backward and gasped, "Did you follow me?"

The wall was cold against her back, the shadows of the room twitching and leaping in tandem with the jerky movements of her flashlight. The shadows of his wings were hulking and large, as if they belonged to a more brutish creature.

Ash stopped his forward progress, but his frown had hardened, his gaze icier than she recalled it ever being before.

*"Did you?"* she snapped.

"I sure as hell didn't come back to reminisce."

She swallowed, her throat sluggish to cooperate. "So, Mr. Kuvaqa was right. You were taken. They brought you here."

As soon as she said the name of his former student, Ash's nostrils flared, and his gaze went from cold to downright hostile.

"What did I say about *dropping it,* Wandern?" The words were forced out through clenched teeth.

Sam didn't move, thinking it might somehow be better if she just stayed still.

"Jesus Christ, you can't leave it alone, can you?" He paced in front of her, his movements slow but not at all safe. Like a lion that was only bored and lazy until a gazelle wandered into its path. "It's like you can't help yourself. No matter how many times I tell you it's dangerous, you don't listen. You go off on your own and do it anyway, consequences be damned."

"Yeah, well, so did you."

Ash came to a stop. He was deathly quiet until he turned his head and looked straight at her.

"Excuse me?"

"The missing children," Sam said, braced against the wall as if it would lend her bravery. "You wouldn't let that go, either—"

He closed the distance between them in two long strides, and his hands braced against the wall on either side, keeping her trapped in place without so much as a touch.

"And look how that turned out." He leaned in closer, the longer strands of his bangs slipping into his face. "I followed the evidence and witness statements, because I thought I was the only one who could help those kids, and guess what? I didn't help them. By the time I got caught and dragged down to this hellhole, most of them were already dead, and the rest—"

His words choked off, sputtered, and died, like a flame smothered on the wick.

"I should have left it alone," he said after a long moment where nothing broke the silence except their scattered breaths. "I should have listened to Kathy and let it be. Those kids never had a chance."

"You didn't know that," Sam said, though she had no real idea what she was saying. Just an inkling of something, a hint from the horror she'd glimpsed through the window. "At least you did something."

He hovered closer. She had nowhere left to retreat.

"Why are you *here?*"

His face twisted, not only in anger, but something jagged and fragile. It was almost enough for her to lose her nerve, for her to say she was sorry. That they could leave now and she wouldn't bring it up again, because all the answers she wanted seem to come at a cost.

She didn't say any of that. What she did say felt like a long time coming.

"Because I don't know anything about you! You won't tell me anything! You won't let me in! I'm trapped in this hell—and even though you're with me, you're not! You're just... somewhere else. And I'm alone." She trembled by the end, adrenaline soaked and suddenly exhausted, her stomach twisting into wretched knots.

"I don't know who you are," she said, her voice barely above a whisper. "I tried to find out for myself, but I still don't know. I don't know who you are, Ash."

He retreated a few inches, and in the shadows cast in the downward angle of the flashlight, it was difficult to see his face. But Sam could feel something different in the dark. A light touch against her cheek, his fingers almost timid as he traced her cheekbone.

"It doesn't matter who I was. That man died a long time ago."

"I don't think that's true." Sam leaned against his hand, forcing the touch to solidify as he held her cheek in his palm. "Why else would you be angry?"

"I'm not—"

She moved her head too far, a mistake, unintentional as her lips brushed against the inside of his wrist.

A shudder went through him so hard she felt it, the leathery ruffle of his wings making it seem like they were in an underground cave filled with bats disturbed from slumber.

But he didn't let her go. Ash's fingers curled into her hair, gripping her, and a jolt shot through her at the tug on her scalp. Now she was the one to tremble, the metallic taste of fear in her mouth. In this place, damp with shadows and mold, the monstrous acts of its previous occupants soaked into the stone in a permanent stain, she finally understood this part of him. The part that was birthed in a buried grave.

The part that watched her with a hunger that seemed without end, through eyes that weren't entirely familiar.

His breath was hot on her face, and his lips grazed her temple as he leaned close to her ear. The single word dragged over a pit of the blackest pitch. It was a warning. A command.

A plea.

*"Run."*

He released her, and Sam bolted.

She only kept a grip on her flashlight because it was still attached to her keys, and the light swung wildly up the stairwell. Sam didn't slow to correct it, to properly light her way; she fled like a deer before a wildfire or a mouse before the tractor.

Lungs burned, legs ached and cramped, but she didn't stop. All she could hear were her panicked breaths, stomping footsteps, and the blood thundering in her ears.

The ascent up the stairwell felt like fleeing out of hell with the devil on her heels, and she didn't slow even when she reached the ground floor and burst outside.

She was confused, disoriented. This wasn't the way she came in. The forest was too close, and where was her car?

Something within the gaping maw of the bunker set her off. A rustle of movement, a flash in the corner of her eye, the animal part of her didn't stop to take a second look.

Sam flew to the trees.

The underbrush was immediately cruel, clawing and scratching at her jeans as she crashed through it. There were no paths or trails here, just a wild forest allowed to slowly encroach on the long-abandoned fort.

The light was fading through the tall, straight trunks of the ponderosa pines. She was going to get lost out here, if she hadn't already, but Sam didn't dare stop, and she didn't dare look behind her.

She didn't need to. She could hear it, or sense it, or maybe even smell it. Whatever it was, it wasn't Ash, not entirely. Her hand throbbed, beckoning to the beast behind her.

Sam liked to think she at least put up a fight, had made a decent attempt to get away, but he caught her with ease. Embarrassing, really, if she was in a mind to care about dignity.

She was wrenched off her feet by an iron grip around her ankle. The pine needles softened her fall, but she still scraped her hands as she tried to crawl and kick out.

Her foot connected with something hard, and she crawled a few paces before she was grabbed by both ankles and yanked backward again.

A hand grabbed the back of her neck and shoved her flat to the ground, and she went still. Warm breath fanned over her shoulder, and she stayed frozen like a rabbit caught in a fox's jaws, hoping to play dead long enough to make a final escape.

But there was no escape. And even if there was, Sam wouldn't have taken it. The throbbing in her hand spread to the rest of her body in a traitorous pulse, though it didn't dampen the fear. If anything, there was a strange feedback loop caught between the fear and arousal, and she didn't know whether to run or to submit.

As if there was a choice. But Sam didn't lay there quietly as her jeans were unbuttoned and tugged off, along with her boots.

Ash yanked off her jacket, and when she was left only in her shirt, she threw back an elbow to throw him off balance.

She barely nudged him. He issued a warning growl in her ear, and with the prickle of claws on her neck, she decided to lie still. In a startling rip, he tore off what remained of her shirt, leaving her exposed to the rapidly dropping temperatures.

And then the molten heat of flesh pressed against her back, and the warmth was so enticing she curled her spine, seeking relief from the chill.

Ash had been assertive when he fed on her before, but this was different. A glimpse of what he might become if he relinquished his humanity.

If he still had control, it was with the barest grip. He held her down as he kneed her legs apart; like an animal in heat, there was no foreplay or intimacy. He nosed along her throat, teeth scraping against her skin as he blindly prodded for what he wanted from her.

*"Ash."*

He paused at the sound of his name, or maybe at the way her voice cracked around it. Could he understand her? Was he aware of what he was doing? Or was he lost to the creature that had him in its grip, just as surely as she was in his.

"Ash," she tried again. "Ash, *please.*"

Sam wasn't begging him to stop, but for a sign he could hear her, that he wasn't completely gone. She knew Ash, or at least she was beginning to. She didn't know this dark-eyed creature that seemed to want to devour her until nothing was left.

After a moment, something brushed against her ear, then her cheek, tickling. His lips tracing her skin, something he'd done before. Something human.

He was still there. Even if he was buried underneath hunger

and horror and a cruel nature he couldn't escape, Ash was there. That was enough for her.

"Okay," she whispered. "It's okay."

She braced her arms against the ground.

The tip of his cock found her entrance, and he slid inside with one hard, smooth snap.

She smothered her cry into her arm. He stretched her so far she thought she might split, but her attempts to pull away were perfunctory. The feel of him was strange, inhuman and overwhelming.

She closed her eyes, trying to adjust, but he didn't give her a chance, one hard thrust following another. She gasped for breath, her body trembling. Her skin was soon slicked with sweat, but not from fear. Even as her hindbrain believed she might just be eaten instead of fucked, Sam trusted Ash. Maybe that was stupid when he wasn't entirely in control, but she did.

And he certainly wasn't in control. His familiar scent, the comforting weight against her back, the way he filled her completely, she found she wanted those things from Ash. But the demon ignored whatever it was she wanted, or didn't want, and simply took.

And it was so, so good. Maybe even better than before. Sam didn't have to quiet herself, didn't have to avoid his eyes before he saw something she didn't want him to see. And he wasn't careful or gentle. He didn't seem to care for her pleasure at all.

That knowledge alone twisted something inside her, made her raise her hips to meet his, her fingers digging into the grass.

She shouldn't be enjoying this, a small part of her thought. He couldn't control himself; he wouldn't be fucking her like this otherwise. A good person wouldn't—

With the next forceful rock of his hips, she forgot all about what a good person was supposed to do, and simply did the only thing she could: remember to breathe so she didn't pass out.

Each thrust threatened to shove her forward, but he kept her in place, one hand still curled around the nape of her neck while the other had her by the wrist. She bit her lip to keep in the animal sounds she was making, but there was no one to hear her except for a hawk and a few straggling elk, and they certainly wouldn't care.

He continued to fuck her like a beast in heat, and she could feel her own slickness coating her thighs, the sound of it obscene in the quiet, though it shouldn't have been. This was primordial, the basest calling, and it certainly wasn't a civilized act.

Sam trembled as her body began to tighten, regretful it was almost over, her back arching so he could rut into her harder. Ash hadn't said a word, he'd barely made any noise, but at her last movement he growled a warning in her ear.

Sam ignored it. She groaned and shivered, her only concern how to take him even deeper. She clenched down on him.

Her goading worked; his pace was brutal, her ass already hurt, and still she braced herself to take all of him.

Perhaps to anchor himself, Ash let go of her wrist, and his palm pressed against the burning symbol on her hand. Fire shot down her arm and into her gut, and she was left breathless.

When she clenched down on him again, this time involuntarily, Ash's movements stuttered and were thrown off rhythm. In a distant part of her mind, she remembered what he'd told her once. He couldn't orgasm until she did, he couldn't chase his own relief. He had to wait for *her.*

That last thought tipped her over the edge, and then a pair of teeth sank into her shoulder.

She couldn't remember much after that. Everything went

hazy white as heat and electricity cascaded over her. A deep pulse resounded through her bones and muscles, chemicals flooding the pathways of her body as something more primitive was taken from her.

It took, and it took, and it continued to take. Sam didn't fight it, even when darkness crept around the edges of her vision. She let him take what he needed from her because it was what he needed.

And she'd never been needed like this before.

CHAPTER FIFTEEN

# SAM

SAM'S FIRST THOUGHT, AS SHE STARED UP AT THE plaster motel ceiling, was that she must have visited one of the bars off the main street the night before. The ache in her pelvis reminded her this was not so.

It took far longer than normal for Sam to roll out of bed, her limbs feeling disjointed and strange. Expecting to be covered with dirt and leaves, she was proven wrong with a glance, her skin relatively clean if marred by the occasional scratch and bruise. Her clothes from the day were folded on a nearby chair, and she wore a long nightshirt, underwear, and sweatpants.

A rush of emotions hit Sam like a storm, pelting her with dangerous debris. Horror at the memories of the bunker, flushed heat at what happened in the forest after, and now a mixture of something she couldn't name. She'd been cleaned, redressed, and carefully deposited into the cheap motel bed.

Mostly, she was irritated. Why did he never stay after? He'd spent a little time with her after the party, but that had only been to make sure she got home safely.

Just like last night.

She got out of bed to check, and yes, her purse was lying on the side table, and her rental car was parked outside when she peeked through the curtains. It was as if last night never happened —but it had, in startling clarity. Each time they did this, Sam's recollection became clearer.

She didn't know *why* it had happened. He'd fed from her only a couple of days before. Her mark hadn't burned, and her body hadn't compelled her to let him feed. Even Ash had seemed normal—angry, certainly, but normal, until she'd pressed her lips against his wrist.

Why had she done that?

She glanced at her phone and hurried to the bathroom; there wasn't much time before she had to check out. There wasn't anything left for her in Aspen Falls, and it felt like a defeat no matter from which angle she viewed it.

She turned on the light to the bathroom and froze. On the sink sat her voice recorder, and underneath was a folded piece of hotel stationery. Sam picked up the paper and carefully flattened it.

All it said was: *Play me.*

Sam lifted the recorder with all the caution of handling a sleeping venomous snake, and hit play.

Static issued from the recorder, along with the shuffle of moving fabric, and then Ash began to speak.

*"Samara. I, uh...I wanted to... Well, an apology isn't going to cut it, is it? But I am sorry. About last night. I didn't..."*

The sound of shuffling again, followed by a sigh.

*"I don't know what to say. Not because I want to withhold anything, I just don't understand what's happening. And that's*

*hard to admit, especially to you. I wish I had more for you than 'I don't know.'"*

Another stretch of silence, but when his voice returned, it held a kind of vague warmth that had Sam pressing the device closer to her ear.

*"I listened to your interview with Lansa. It was good to hear his voice after all these years. Strange to think he's older than me now. I wish he didn't feel guilty. He's wrong. What happened to me wasn't his fault."*

It was quiet, but she was close enough to the recorder to catch the small intake of breath.

*"You came all this way for answers. It would be a shame to let you go back without any, even if I think flying across the country to trespass on government property was a reckless way to do it. I can't fault you for the pursuit of knowledge, not when I would preach the same thing to my kids.*

*"I'll tell you everything, Samara. Or at least, what I can remember. You deserve that much."*

Sam dressed and packed up her meager belongings. When she checked out of her room, she ignored the scandalized look from the same woman who had checked her in. Sam wouldn't be surprised if she'd spotted Ash carrying her unconscious to her room. She didn't care what the woman thought.

All she could focus on was the recorder burning a hole through her pocket. As soon as she stopped at a gas station on the outskirts of town and grabbed a few snacks that would serve as a paltry road breakfast, Sam plugged the aux cable into the recorder.

Wanting as few driving distractions as possible, she waited until she was on the highway before she reached over to the passenger seat, and once again, hit the play button.

*Lansa was wrong about one thing, and right about another. I had heard about the missing kids before he mentioned anything about it. Being so close to the reservation, with a lot of relatives on either side of the boundary, our communities used to be a lot closer than they seem to be now.*

*So I already knew about the disappearances from other faculty and word of mouth. It was one of those topics that folks would talk around without actually delving into. It's a kind of dissonance that's hard to describe unless you've lived in that kind of insular community.*

*Anyway, Lansa was right about the catalyst. His cousin's disappearance hit him hard, and I just couldn't sit around and wait for more kids to vanish. No one would talk about it, no one would say it aloud, but we knew where the kids were going.*

*The base in the mountain valley was relatively new. No one knew why they'd built a military fort in the middle of the mountains. There was no strategic value in the location, except that it was remote and hard to get to.*

*The only reason you were able to get in so easily is because the government removed most of the barricades and walls when they closed the fort. They figured the radiation warnings would keep out curious hikers and urban explorers. Noticed the lack of graffiti inside? Yeah, it worked, for most people. Guess they weren't prepared for someone with your level of persistent, bullheaded curiosity.*

*And before you get annoyed—yes, I can say that, because I was the same way, and that's how I got into the shitstorm I did. My sister and I knew those trails better than even the forest rangers, and I used that knowledge to bypass the perimeter fences and patrols.*

*All I wanted was proof. I thought if I could snap a few pictures and show what they were doing required an outside investigation, it would be enough to lead to the kids. Everyone in town knew it wasn't a normal base. Whatever they were doing at the fort knocked out the entire power grid at least once a month, and there were lots of stories about strange lights coming from the mountains.*

*I thought it was embellishment on its way to becoming an urban legend. Who doesn't love a story about dubious military experiments hidden away from public scrutiny? Except it wasn't a story, and there was no satisfying conclusion where the children are saved and the plucky protagonist goes home a hero.*

*Instead, the nosy idiot gets caught, thrown into a cage, and finds out what really happened to the kids. There was no saving them by then.*

*There are two main kinds of demons: those who are parasitic, and those who are predatory. They both feed from humans, and the main difference between them is one leaves their prey alive, and you can guess what happens to the other.*

*Most demons in popular media are the parasitic kind. They leave their host alive, because like any parasite in the animal kingdom, it's more beneficial to keep your food source breathing. Still, some parasites do eventually kill their host, and they have to infect another before that happens, otherwise they die along with them. Technically, it's a symbiotic relationship, albeit an unhealthy, one-sided type of deal.*

*Predatory demons are nearly unheard of, mainly because they don't leave witnesses or bodies. They're stalkers, hunters, and ambushers. Meticulous, violent, and thankfully, extremely rare.*

*There are folks who know of the existence of demons and hunt them. Demons don't die, not really. Kill a demon, and they return to their realm. Some of them are content to stay there, while others will snatch any weakness between the worlds and find their way back. No one really knows why. Demons don't need to feed in their realm—they have all the sustaining energy they need there, but once they get a taste of humans, most of them would do anything to keep feeding from humans. It's a hard thing to describe. Addiction seems too mild.*

*Anyway, the assholes at the base were using a portal to the demonic realm to try to infect the kids with demonic energy.*

*I don't know where the portal came from, where it is now, or if it's been destroyed, but at the time, they used it. At least they never opened it fully, thank God. The thing acted like a camera lens with a shutter, and they only opened the aperture a little at a time, just enough to capture the energy that came through.*

*I don't know why they picked children. Easier to control, maybe. Less likely to fight back. Maybe they thought it would be easier for the demonic energy to take root in a child.*

*Whatever the reason, from what I could see from my cage, it wasn't working.*

*I thought they were going to kill me. They certainly beat the hell out of me and only stopped when they realized I really didn't know anything. No one had sent me. I wasn't a foreign spy or internal saboteur. I was just some asshole science teacher who didn't have the wisdom to stay home.*

*It would have been better if they had killed me. Instead, they strapped me down, pumped me so full of drugs I thought I was back in the 1960s again, and then they blasted me with whatever the fuck kind of cosmic radiation exists in the demon realm.*

*I don't know the exact science of how it works. Hell, the people who did this to me said more than once they weren't sure why it worked on me either. But it did. I don't remember much, just that everything hurt, and I was scared. That's the gist of it.*

*And there you go. I'm the only successful asset that came out of Project Pointfall. They knew just enough about demon-making to carve my* signum *before I could break free. It sealed me to my—at the time they called him a "handler," but he was the master, and I was the slave. Everything belonged to him, even my mind.*

*It doesn't take a genius to see why the military would want demonically enhanced soldiers. They could have fully opened the portal and simply enslaved whatever demon came through, but well, the optics of the United States government using demons as soldiers would be a little too much for the good Christian taxpayers to swallow.*

*The problem with Project Pointfall was, after two decades, I was the only successful thing that came out of their little horror show. Even so, they put me to use.*

*You can imagine what that was. Assassinations. Precise, surgical attacks. Undercover subterfuge once I learned how to use my aspect. They didn't always want a target eliminated. Sometimes, they wanted information. Who better to send than an incubus that can seduce the target and erase all memory that he was even there?*

*Whatever they wanted, I did, and I did it well, but General Vogel wanted an army. And you can't make an army out of one guy, no matter how well he fights or fucks his targets.*

*They wanted more soldiers, and even though they'd failed in the past, they decided to try again using children.*

*I took them. So many of them from all over the world, from places they wouldn't be missed—as if such a place could exist. As if someone wouldn't mourn them. And if they didn't have family to mourn them, I did. Even though my humanity was buried deep under my demon skin, I knew what I was doing and who I was doing it to.*

*I never failed my missions, not even the ones that seemed impossible. But there was one mission I couldn't complete. One child I couldn't take. So, I didn't.*

*The punishment was severe, and I would have accepted it like I had taken all of the other shit they did to me. But when the General said they would send agents to her house, slaughter her family, stage it to look like a home invasion, and take her regardless—I snapped.*

*I killed almost everyone. That's when the bureaucrats found out about the secret project. Of course, they swept it under the rug, but they also shut it down permanently which I only discovered later, because I died that day—gunned down by the lab security team.*

*But the thing is with demons, they don't stay dead. I went to the place all demons go when they're banished from this plane of existence.*

*I don't know how long I was there. Four? Five years? That's according to Earth time, which I'm fairly sure doesn't correlate to demonic time in a way that makes sense, because to me, it was one long eternity of sandblasted, red-tinted Hell.*

*Until well, you know the rest. You brought me back. And I don't know if it was fate, or if you have the worst luck of anyone I've ever met, but I can tell you, I was shocked to find the kid who freed me was the same one I had refused to take.*

*I don't know how they picked the kids. I don't know why they picked you. But you can see why I didn't want to tell you. Why that* signum *on your hand is one of the worst things that could have happened to you. It still might be.*

*This is probably a cold comfort, but I'm closer to getting an answer, and hopefully, a solution to fix it.*

*That's pretty much the long and the short of it. It's weird, I haven't talked this much since the last class I taught. Forgot how exhausting it is, but in a good way.*

*It's getting late, and I should probably go before some deputy decides to ask why I'm sitting in your car. I think you're still asleep, but I'll check on you one last time before I leave the recorder.*

*I hope this gives you some of what you were looking for. I would have preferred to do it in person, but well. Can't exactly trust myself not to...yeah.*

*This recording is yours to do with as you wish. You can delete it or keep it. Most of the people involved are dead, including me, so it's not like anyone can verify the information. Just be careful. Okay? That's...that's all I ask.*

*Have a safe flight, and I'll see you soon.*

## CHAPTER SIXTEEN

# SAM

It was as if Sam's life had been split in two: life before Arizona, and life after.

Her road trip back to Phoenix and her return flight to Seattle had been almost dreamlike. She'd bought noise-cancelling headphones at the airport just to replay the recording. Combined with the expense of the plane tickets and motel room, she would be eating noodles for a while, but it had been worth it.

It wasn't the words she focused on during the flight—she'd heard them enough times to begin to memorize them. It was Ash's voice she absorbed, the cadence of his storytelling, the easy rhythm he fell into when he spoke about a topic he understood well.

He was comforting. Her heart hadn't raced once during the flight, even when they picked up turbulence somewhere over the Mojave Desert. Sam simply closed her eyes and pretended he was there, speaking to her, giving her the answers he'd withheld.

She didn't resent his choice to keep her in the dark. Instead, her heart ached at the knowledge he'd carried this burden alone.

That night, when she crawled into bed, Ash's words were on

her mind. When she woke and got ready for work, they were still there. The longer Sam thought about it, the more certain she became that she could help him. She just didn't know how yet. And she certainly didn't know what to do with the information she'd been given. Some of the strangeness of her childhood began to make sense, moments when she was sure something was wrong, that her nightmares were more than just fragments of fiction.

But as she got older, the nightmares eased and eventually stopped. The creeping shadows, the rotting bears, the dark figures over her bed, they no longer haunted her, and until recently, she'd forgotten she'd once had such dreams.

Sam still had no memories of any portals, or demons, and she certainly didn't remember Ash with any real clarity. She only remembered sitting cramped in the closet with her Ouija board long after her friends lost interest in trying to communicate with the dead. It made Sam angry; of course they didn't care about ghosts. They weren't actually trying to talk to someone. Sam was.

And apparently, something had answered. It just hadn't been her father.

Work dragged on, as it always did, and several times a day she checked her phone for a missed call or text. Nothing.

She was desperate to talk to Ash, but no matter how much she wanted to pick up her phone and just call him, she didn't.

What would she say? That her stomach had twisted into knots as he'd shared the horrific things he'd experienced? How she'd had to pull her car off the highway, her vision too blurry to see, as he recounted the horrific things he'd been forced to do?

He'd been tortured because they couldn't stamp out the decency and kindness he'd managed to hold onto. They'd *killed* him because he finally told them "No."

How was she supposed to say "I'm sorry" to that?

There it was, that sliver of guilt needling under her skin. He'd sacrificed himself for a kid he didn't even know. And now, he was stuck with her. Truly, no good deed went unpunished.

Sam left her phone where it was. They would be forced together in a few days, and until then, he deserved some peace. She could give him that much. She owed him much more.

The rest of the week passed, and Sam finished her last workday for the year. The office was closed on Christmas, but she'd saved her vacation days to take off all the way until New Year's.

With absolutely no plans for the next few days, Sam was going to sleep in, avoid contact with people—especially her coworkers who most likely thought her an alcoholic since her boss's party—and think.

She missed the warmth of Arizona. Even the coldness of the White Mountains didn't hold the biting frigidness of the north.

She missed the feel of the small town, nestled in the dark arms of the mountainous forest. What she'd found had been terrifying, but it hadn't been all bad. She recalled the gift shop with a certain fondness, as well as her time with Mr. Kuvaqa.

Mostly, she missed Ash. She could pretend she enjoyed the emptiness of her apartment and schedule, that her solitude was all she craved. And that would have been true, in the before. But she was in the after, now. And everything was different this side of Arizona.

Pulling the key fob out of her purse, she held the collar of her jacket against the chilled air of the garage and fled into the protection of her car. Once inside, she turned the key...and nothing happened.

She tried again. The engine didn't make a sound, didn't even attempt to turn over, and the overhead lights were lifeless and dark.

"Shit!"

She slammed her palm against the steering wheel, but the car remained ambivalent to her anger, and now she had a throbbing hand as well as a dead car.

As soon as she opened the door she regretted it, every inch of exposed skin burned from the cold, and she could barely think, let alone call a ride service.

She fled up the elevator and back to the warmth of the office. Jaw clenched, she pulled out her phone. Her nearest relative was hours away, the trains didn't run near her apartment, and in the years she'd lived in the city, she'd somehow managed to avoid making any close friends. Her neighbors and coworkers were acquaintances at best. She had no one to reach out to.

Except, she did.

The home screen was open, and her finger hovered over Contacts instead of the ride share app. She tapped it, and the first name listed was *Ash.*

It made sense, his name began with A, after all, but her stomach still flipped in a confusing acrobatic display.

Sam couldn't call him for this. It had nothing to do with *that* side of her life. Plus, she would feel like an asshole if the first time she reached out was to ask him for a favor. And it seemed rude to ask him to drive through dangerous whiteout conditions because she couldn't afford to replace her old, cheap car.

She closed the contact list despite knowing it might be her last hope. Who would be giving rides in this weather?

"Oh, hey, Sam. You good?"

Sam stiffened so fast something creaked in her spine. She turned, stiff, robotic, and Davin gave her a dazzling smile.

*Oh, you've got to be shitting me—*

"Thought you'd be gone by now," he prompted, oblivious to her blank stare.

"Yeah." She was too tired to try to hide her exhaustion. "Well, no. I mean, my battery died. And with the weather this bad, I'm just going to call someone."

His frown was a sympathetic pantomime.

"Why don't I give you a ride? Save whoever you were going to call a trip."

She glanced down at her phone. He had a point, and hadn't she just thought the same thing?

"Uh, thanks," she said, the excuse already weak on her lips, "but I don't want to be an inconvenience—"

"I don't mind."

Sam squeezed her phone as if it was a lifeline, but it remained silent in her hand.

"It's the least I can do for being such an ass at the party," he added.

Her resolve gave way with a dreadful, inevitable descent, like a trapped creature in a tarpit. "Yeah, okay."

He sounded sincere, and despite her recent paranoia, there had been a time when she liked him. There must have been a reason for it, even if the reasons dangled out of her reach now. "Thanks."

"No problem," he said, flashing his usual bright smile. "Like I said, it's the least I can do."

Sam tried not to drag her feet as she followed Davin into the elevator.

*It'll be fine,* she told herself as the clunky machine made its descent. *Let him do the nice guy thing. He'll feel better about the party, and he'll stop thinking he owes you any favors.*

And she would make it home much faster this way. Win-win all around. Maybe the night could be salvaged, after all.

His car was black, sleek, and low profile. It was an upgrade from her cheap ride, as evidenced by the seat that heated pleasantly underneath her. Davin eased the car out of the parking garage and drove the cramped downtown streets in silence, the radio turned down to such a soft volume that, while music played, the song remained a mystery. The sight of her building perked up her mood, and she wondered why she'd been so reluctant to begin with. Davin was overbearing and strange, but he was harmless.

"I'm sorry again, really," he said after he stopped close to the entrance. His eyes were round and sincere as he leaned toward her, one hand resting on the back of her seat. "I realize I've been coming on strong lately, and I thought it best if I cleared the air."

All of Sam's goodwill deflated like a punctured balloon.

"It's fine, really." Screw that stupid, dumbass little voice that said this was a good idea. *Just let me get out of the damn car.* "I shouldn't have snapped at you. Thanks for the—"

"I really like you, you know?"

He released a sigh and ran his fingers through his hair. Sam was a frozen deer before a freight train. Her mind screamed at her to grab the handle and yank the door open, but she didn't move.

"Ever since the Halloween party, I feel like, I dunno. Like I want to get to know you better."

*Stop talking. Please, stop talking.*

"Oh?"

Sam leaned toward the door, as far as her body would take her toward escape.

"Yeah," he continued, expression serious. It was like there were two entirely different conversations going on, and Sam wasn't a true participant in either one. "I feel like we have this connection, Sam."

He leaned closer across the middle console, breaching her personal space, and his eyes were riveted, intense in a way they shouldn't be. Making eye contact wasn't unusual for Davin, he never had a short supply of confidence, but this was a new kind of focus. Sharp. Hungry.

Sam yanked open the door handle and stumbled from the car. She yelled back a hasty, "thanks for the ride!" and slammed the door in his face.

The brutal chill was a welcome relief from the suffocating air in the car, and she hurried to her building. The hairs on the nape of her neck stood straight as she listened for the crunch of footsteps behind her, but there was nothing. As she entered the lobby, the glare of headlights moved past her and vanished down the street.

Sam kept going on legs that trembled, her heart thundering in her ears. She skipped the elevator and climbed the steps so quickly she was panting by the time she hit the landing, and she fumbled the keys in her lock. She kept checking the hallway behind her, but she was alone.

Finally, she turned the key and rushed inside, locking it shut and backing away from the door as if it might spring open on its own. Something brushed against her leg, and she jumped with a yelp.

The cat at her feet was unbothered, his meow impatient and hungry.

"Oh," she exhaled a breath. "Thanks for the heart attack, little shithead."

He screamed happily in reply.

She went through the motions of feeding Monster, and then

she pulled off her shoes and perched on the edge of her couch cushion, attempting to rub the stress from her face.

Sam hadn't imagined things. Davin, who had politely ignored her for most of the time they'd worked together, had developed some kind of fixation on her ever since Ash had arrived in her life. It wasn't a coincidence.

Did he know, somehow? He couldn't. At least, not consciously. Was there some kind of side effect to having sex with an incubus? Something that affected those around her?

It was the only thing she could think of, and she would have to ask Ash the next time she saw him. Unintentionally seducing Davin by proxy was far more likely than him taking a genuine interest in her. As much as Sam liked to believe she was that likeable, she had too much self-awareness for that. There was a reason the people she could call for a ride were on a short list.

At least she wouldn't have to worry about Davin for another two weeks—

A series of thuds struck her door.

*"I know you're in there!"* shouted a voice. *"Saw you walk past!"*

Mr. Morris. Sam had slammed her door again.

Sam unlocked and opened her door, and before she could open her mouth, his tirade had already started.

"That damn cat!" he snarled, his weathered face beet red. "I know you got one in there! It was howlin' and scratchin' at the walls not five minutes ago!"

"I don't have a cat, Mr. Morris. It must have been someone else."

His eyes narrowed. The bastard recognized a placating customer service voice when he heard it, and he wasn't about to let it appease him today.

"My eyes might be goin', but my hearin' is just fine. And I know what a goddamn *cat* sounds like."

A fact he loved to remind Sam of on a daily basis, typically with angry banging on their shared wall.

"I heard your animal, I know I did! Thought it was going to rip a hole through your door." His face screwed up like he'd bitten into a lemon. "Keep down the noise, I said, but you don't listen. Don't think I won't call the landlord—"

"That's your prerogative."

If his face twisted anymore, it was liable to pop off.

"The leasing office has been through my apartment before," Sam said with an even hand, although hers were feeling particularly violent at the moment, "and they've found nothing. You're more than welcome to demand they do it again, as I'm sure they'll appreciate being told how to run their building."

His squint was that of someone used to getting their way and coming to the impossible conclusion they were being denied.

"Maybe I will," he said with a curl of his lips. "And I'm going to find proof of that damn cat."

With a turn of his heels, Mr. Morris stomped back to his apartment, causing more noise than Monster could possibly make.

Sam shut her door with too much strength, and several seconds later, another heavy knock thudded against its surface.

She threw open the door, teeth bared for an impending argument, and a hand gripped her throat and shoved her back into the apartment.

The strength forcing her backwards was inhuman, and a scream was trapped in her lungs as she hit the wall with a hard thud.

Green eyes filled her vision, along with lips pulled over teeth in a predator's smile.

"Well. That was easy."

Davin kicked the door shut, the force of it enough to rattle the wood in its jamb.

"What's with the look?" He jerked her forward, pulling her into the living room. "Aren't you happy to see me, Sammy?"

She dragged her feet against the carpet, her denial coming out as a small, animal noise.

Davin thew her forward; she put out her hands to break her fall, but not fast enough. The edge of the coffee table hit her temple, stars bursting in her vision.

The world spun in constellations and confusion. She tried to crawl away, fingers digging into the carpet, but her body was sluggish. When Davin grabbed her shoulder and rolled her onto her back, she had no strength to fight.

He grabbed her by the chin and tilted her head, clicking his tongue in disapproval. Something warm trickled down her head into her hair.

"So fragile," he mused. "It's a wonder you're not extinct."

Sam opened her mouth, terror bubbling underneath the pain, but he dug his fingers into her jaw.

"Shhh," he cooed, expression full of mocking pity. "It'll be over soon. It only hurts for a while, and then it's so much better. Don't you want that? Aren't you tired of being all alone, with no one who cares what becomes of you?"

His grip tightened and forced her mouth wider. Sam jerked back, but the power in his fingers was as undeniable as the strength he'd used to force his way into her apartment.

She kicked at him, and he batted away her leg like he was swatting a fly. When she tried a second time, he forced her legs still and straddled her, sitting on her stomach. He trapped her arms underneath his legs, immobilizing her.

She couldn't move, could barely breathe, and her mind was just as trapped as her body, repeating an endless cycle of: *Why? Why? Why?*

"None of that. Come on, open up." Davin's hold on her jaw had slipped during the struggle, and his face twisted into an ugly scowl when Sam kept her mouth tightly shut. "It's only going to hurt more if you fight it."

She shook her head, a denial and an attempt to thrash. Sam's head throbbed, and her ears were ringing as the dim lights of the living room flared too bright.

Davin huffed and pushed down on her chin with his thumb, forcing his fingers between her teeth, holding her mouth open so she couldn't bite. He leaned down to hover over her face, and for a moment, she thought he would kiss her.

In hindsight, that would have been preferable.

Davin opened his mouth wide, and something thick and yellow came up his throat and snaked past his lips. Its hard body was segmented like a centipede, and it was covered with dozens of barbed hooks that flexed in and out of its carapace.

Sam writhed and twisted, trying to turn away, but Davin held her constricted. The thing moved past her teeth and over her tongue, unpleasantly warm, coated in viscous ooze. It tasted like raw, rancid meat.

She screamed.

The thing moved down her throat, cutting off her air and choking her into silence. Her vision blurred—both from tears and a lack of oxygen.

Her gag reflex engaged as soon as the thing touched her throat, and a sizzling noise rose, like meat left on a fryer. Davin gave a muffled shriek. The thing jerked out of her throat, cutting her flesh, and disappeared back down Davin's throat.

Sam coughed and gagged, heaving onto her side as her throat burned. Iron filled her mouth, and red blood dripped onto the carpet.

The *signum* seemed intent on charring her alive, searing along the tattoo lines as if touched by hot iron. Sam screamed and clutched her hand to her chest, pressing down, desperate to extinguish the flames. It had never hurt like this before.

Davin no longer pinned her down; he lay on the floor next to her, also gagging and holding his neck, but his eyes were focused on her. The venomous green stare fell to the hand cradled against her chest.

He was on her in an instant, grabbed her hand, and yanked it away from her body.

She tried to resist, blindly pushing at him, her head spinning, throat so swollen she nearly gagged again.

Davin extended her arm the rest of the way, fingers digging into her wrist so hard she feared it would snap. The brand on the back of her hand flared bright orange as if about to ignite.

The twisted expression on his face barely human, he spit out a word that definitely wasn't.

A fist banged on her door three times in an angry procession. *"What did I say about the goddamn noise!"*

Davin glared at Sam, cold and alien.

She shook her head, tried to tell him, *don't, he's just an ornery old man, don't hurt him,* but she choked, and blood trickled down her mouth. Nothing would move past her ruined throat.

Davin pointed a finger at her face. "Don't fucking move. Don't make a sound. Do as I say, and I won't break his neck."

Sam nodded.

Davin rose to his feet and went to the door, yanking it open and glaring at the neighbor on her doorstep.

Sam groped her pockets until her fingers gripped the flat rectangle against her hip. She pulled out her phone and tried to unlock it, but it wouldn't accept her shaking fingertip. It demanded a password.

Sam coughed up another mouthful of blood, tears wetting the temples of her hair.

"Where is she?" Mr. Morris's voice drifted from the entryway. "I told her to stop making—"

"She's busy. Go the fuck away." Davin slammed the door in his face.

Sam tapped the screen, missed the right numbers. She tried again, and the screen unlocked. Jabbing open the contacts list, her phone shook violently in her hands, but she held on.

Just as she touched the name *Ash,* the phone vanished from her hands.

Davin's lips pulled into a snarl, and he snapped her phone in half. "Who were you calling, huh? Your master?"

The sneer was laden with disdain, his poisonous glare equally disgusted. "I sure as hell know you're not calling anyone else. Such an isolated little thing. Pathetically, utterly alone. Is that why you made a bargain?"

Sam rolled onto her stomach and crawled between the couch and coffee table. Something hard slammed into her ribs, and she curled into a fetal position to protect herself.

"All that fucking work!"

Another kick to her side. She cried in agonized silence.

"All of it, *gone!*"

She scrambled away, but he was right behind her; he grabbed an ankle and yanked her back as she clawed the carpet.

"Do you know how long it took me to get this close! *Years!*"

He gripped the front of her throat. "And then I get here, only to find you're some demon's whore!"

Sam scrabbled at his hold, but he jerked her upward, arching her spine painfully.

He growled low in her ear. "No doubt your master is on its way."

His breath ghosted across her face, and she tried to wrench free, disgust and fear clearing the pain in her head. But the creature that wore Davin's face held on tight.

"I'm going to leave you in fucking pieces for it to find. I sincerely hope it feels the exact moment I rip out your heart. In fact, I'm sure it will."

He squeezed until her air was gone.

Sam twitched, involuntary, harder with each passing heartbeat. She clawed at his arms, her nails digging into flesh, and it was as if she clawed at nothing.

A yowl filled the room, and Davin screamed. He thew her forward, and she hit the carpet hard enough for her vision to spin. She thought she was imagining Monster on Davin's shoulder, sinking claws and teeth into flesh, ripping through his jacket to the skin underneath, but it was enough to get her stumbling to her feet.

Davin lifted her cat by the back of his neck and flung him hard. He hit the wall with enough force to leave a crack in the plaster.

Fury roared through her. Sam grabbed what was closest and launched at Davin. The table lamp in her hands crashed into the back of his head.

He didn't flinch. Davin turned, pupils pulled into pinpricks so small all she could see was an expanse of bright green.

The ember of rage within her died. She stumbled, her numb legs carrying her until her back hit the wall.

He moved slowly and languidly, an unhurried predator. His lips parted, and not one, but three of the insect-like segments pushed up from his throat, spreading as if in monstrous bloom.

Sam's stomach seized, and she surveyed the room for something, *anything* she could use to fight.

The appendages pulled back, poised as if to aim, and shot toward her face.

She recoiled and shut her eyes, but there was only silence.

She opened her eyes. The barbed ends of the appendages hovered inches from her face. Past them, Davin choked as an arm curled around his neck, a pair of wings splayed above him, filling the entire room.

The black pits of the eyes and the bared teeth near Davin's neck were faintly familiar. A glimpse in Arizona, of something that wasn't Ash at all.

Segments of the creature curled back toward Ash, and without easing his chokehold, he gripped one of the appendages that strayed too close and gave it a vicious yank.

With a sound like a lobster's shell being cracked, the limb broke off and foul fluid spewed from the wound, spraying ribbons of black onto the carpet.

A putrid stench filled the room, the rancid meat smell pervading the air, but finally, *finally,* Davin's struggles weakened until he was completely still.

Ash kept his grip for a few moments before releasing his hold, dropping the creature onto the floor in a limp heap. He spotted Monster nearby, fur puffed and harried, and Ash pointed at Davin.

"Watch him."

As if he'd been trained for it, Monster leapt onto Davin's back and sat on his haunches, giving a warning growl to his fallen charge.

Sam watched all of this from very far away, distantly aware as her knees buckled, and she slid down the wall. She didn't make it far; Ash picked her up and carried her to the couch.

Even through the numbness trapping her in a hazy fog, Sam couldn't take her eyes off Davin. The limbs, or appendages, or whatever they were, had retracted as soon as he'd passed out. He looked like he did every day at the office, aside from the black smears on his lips and the ghastly pallor of his skin.

"He's not dead."

Ash's voice was stern but his fingers gentle as they touched her face. His hands were rough with callouses, but the texture of it felt clarifying. Grounding in the fog in which she was losing her way.

"He's unconscious," he added. "I need you to look at me."

The words floated past her, undisturbed like the still water of a pond. Ash sighed.

"He's not a demon, if that's what you're worried about." Ash glanced over his shoulder at the subject in question. "But he is possessed by one."

Her vision swam, as unreliable as her thoughts. This couldn't be real. It couldn't be happening.

Ash's voice drifted through the haze. "We don't have a lot of time. I need you to focus, sweetheart. Look at me."

Sam dragged her gaze from Davin's crumbled body, finding Ash's face. At some point, he'd knelt between her knees, his hands resting on her sides and holding her steady.

The hard lines of his brows softened, and the palm of his hand cradled her cheek. "That's it. Keep your eyes on me."

He tilted her face to one side, not far enough to break eye contact, and he examined the warm, sticky mess at her temple.

"It's not deep," he observed. "I'm more worried about a concussion. Stay right here, okay? I'm not going anywhere."

Sam tried to respond, but nothing came out. He frowned but rose to his feet and dug into his jeans pocket, pulling out a flip phone. He opened it, pressed a thumb across the keypad twice, and put it to his ear.

"It's me," he said so quickly Sam didn't know how the line had time to connect. "Put Lazuli on. Now."

His face grew tight from whatever was said on the other end.

*"Demonic possession,* how's that for urgent? Yeah, I'll hold."

Ash's tail swished like a provoked cat about to leap on a mouse, his focus on Davin, loathing etched around his eyes and mouth.

Sam shuddered, her skin growing cold as if the temperature had dropped several degrees. Ash pulled off his jacket and wrapped it around her shoulders, the agitation on his features replaced by a kind of beseeching concern.

Her teeth chattered, or at least she thought they did, her body trying to float away like an untethered balloon. The jacket helped, his scent and lingering body heat keeping her grounded.

Her throat. There was something wrong with her throat. She should tell him, probably, but she was so tired. Everything was strange and far away, even him.

Ash frowned and looked her over more closely as his tail coiled and undulated. He opened his mouth, but his attention was drawn back to his phone.

"Yeah, I'm here. Going to need an extraction team for a possession, and a cleanup crew. It left a mess, and it's possible local authorities have been called."

*Extraction team? Cleanup crew?*

Sam tried to focus on his words, delivered with clipped, professional precision, but they kept drifting away, slipping through her grip like water through her fingers.

"Jesus, I don't know the exact altitude," he growled at whatever was said on the other end. "It's the fourth floor. Probably forty-five to forty-nine feet from the ground—Yeah, fine, just be quick."

Ash snapped the phone shut and shoved it back into his pocket.

The conversation piqued Sam's curiosity, but her throat was an open fire. She swallowed convulsively as she looked at the figure on the floor. The inky black substance surrounded him in a puddle, seeping into the carpet and probably staining the base flooring. Sam wondered if it would leak through the ceiling of the apartment below.

*At least there's a cleanup crew coming.*

Her focus was unblinking, and at times unseeing, until Ash knelt before her and placed warm hands on her arms. His lips were drawn into a severe line, but the angles of his brow were strange, almost timid.

"I know you're in shock, and you'll probably be in a lot of pain soon if you're not already, but this is important. We don't have a lot of time."

Sam blinked some of the film away, and when her ruined throat nearly choked her in a new spasm when she tried to speak, she nodded instead.

Ash chewed his bottom lip, and Sam realized it wasn't timidity in his eyes. It was guilt.

"They can't know," he said. "About the mark. The feedings. The...the sex. They can't know any of it."

He leaned forward and took the hand that carried its heavy burden. The mark was no longer aglow with angry embers and had faded back into intricate lines of pink. Ash pulled off his gloves and slipped them over both of her hands.

"You know who and what I am, because I stopped the *Alp* that night from feeding on you. They...They'll wonder why I didn't take your memory, but I'll handle that. Do you understand?"

No. *No,* she *didn't* understand, but it wasn't within her grasp to say. With every passing minute, she grew colder, her limbs becoming deadweight as her eyes fought to stay open.

She bobbed her head in what might have been agreement or simply a struggle to stay conscious.

As if she were made of glass, he cupped her cheek in his hand. The warmth of it burned against her freezing skin, and she leaned into his palm and let her eyelids slip shut.

"Samara?"

Ash spoke her name, repeated it louder, but she only leaned further into his hand. She liked when he said her name. Always Samara, never Sam. But she didn't like how he said it now, tight and strained. As if he were afraid.

Why was she so cold?

His fingers pushed into her hair as his hands pressed against her cheek, or...no, her head was drooping. Ash was trying to hold her up. But she continued to slip forward until his arms were around her, and he lifted her against something solid and alive with warmth.

Sam curled against it, the trembling worse, accompanied by a sense of numbness starting inside her throat—it no longer ached, but she couldn't seem to swallow.

Ash spoke, but the words trickled past her awareness. Her

mind couldn't process his words. She only heard his panicked tone.

Something in the room changed. The light behind her eyelids glowed, and there was a low thrum that plucked along her nerves. She cracked open her eyes and found something that shouldn't exist: a glowing yellow vertical line in the air, growing longer with each second.

A searing noise rent the air as the line expanded into an oval, ripping open and slicing through the end of her couch.

A boy stepped through, the sight of him so peculiar he couldn't be real. He wore a dark blue cape, with robes made of gold and white cloth, the fabric shimmering when the light reflected off its surface.

The boy glanced her way, a questioning dip to his brows before his focus moved on to the rest of the room.

"Well, you weren't kidding about the mess," he spoke with a lightness that rubbed counter to the disastrous situation.

"Where are the healers?" Ash growled from somewhere above her. "She needs medical attention. *Now.*"

More people spilled through the opening, their robes muted earthly colors in contrast to the circus flare of the boy's.

The boy ignored the newcomers and, instead, peered at Sam more closely. "Heigore venom," he assessed with a frown. "Far too much for an infestation. He overdosed her. Why?"

"Figure it out later." Ash shifted her in his arms. "I'm taking her to the Tower."

"Now, hold on—"

Ash stalked past the boy and headed for the strange, glowing...

*Aperture,* Sam's mind supplied with faint triumph, as if she'd rediscovered a lost word.

And then fear broke through her freezing numbness, and she croaked. *"Mon..."*

Blood bubbled up her throat. *"Mon...sssh...ter..."*

Ash stopped. "Christ's sake—*beast,* get over here!"

There was an answering meow, and something heavy and gray landed on her stomach. Her cat pushed his face against Sam's neck and mewled, a kittenish noise he'd never made before.

She tried to wrap her arms around his furry body, but they wouldn't move. Her head wouldn't rise from where it rested against Ash's shoulder. Her skull weighed a thousand pounds, and the rest of her body was just as heavy. Uttering her cat's name had taken the last of her strength.

"Hold on," Ash said, her only warning before he stepped through the tear in the world.

The journey passed in an instant, but Sam's stomach roiled as if an elevator suddenly ascended. Her skin rippled in goosebumps, the air shifting and changing, and she knew, without knowing how, that she was simply somewhere else.

Monster leapt off her stomach, but the weight on Sam's chest remained dull and heavy. Reedy sprigs of air wheezed out of her throat.

Hands grasped her—not Ash's, but someone else's. Sam wanted to scream, to fight them off. The segmented appendages wrapped around her arms and legs, cinching tight around her neck.

A vicious snarl came from somewhere close to her head, following by shouting and confusion. A woman yelled, *"Spiros, stop! They're trying to help!"*

The vise around her body tightened, suffocating, drowning, pulling her down, and Ash called her name across the inky blackness of nowhere.

# CHAPTER SEVENTEEN

# SAM

WARMTH. SOFT, GENTLE AND PERMEATING, LIKE A soothing bath after being lost in a blizzard.

But Sam wasn't submerged in water. Silky cotton lay under her fingertips, her body horizontal, and her head propped by a pillow that felt like it was spun from a cloud.

She opened her eyes, though it took several failed attempts, and the expectation of waking in her bedroom made her surroundings all the more jarring.

Exotic tapestries of blue and silver lined dark panels of wooded walls. Faded, lavish blue carpet runners stretched across the polished stone floor. And in the center of one wall sat a large writing desk that probably weighed several hundred pounds. In the air floated a faint hint of citrus incense and the scent of old wood and stone.

The bed she occupied was a four-poster, adorned with blue-and-silver brocaded curtains which were tied back, giving her a view of the palatial surroundings.

She was still wearing her clothes, along with Ash's jacket and his gloves. But when she tried to lift the covers to assess the rest of herself, there was resistance along one arm.

Something gray and sinewy wrapped around her wrist, curled carefully, but firmly, around the narrowest point.

Ash's tail.

The demon himself occupied a cerulean armchair next to the bed, head propped on his shoulder, his arms loosely crossed over his chest while he slept.

Sam stared at him for a while, struggling to put the puzzle pieces together, though after a time, her mind quieted and she simply watched. Ash was peaceful, serene in sleep. Strands of dark hair draped over his face, the lines of his forehead smooth and untroubled.

Had he waited there for Sam to awaken?

As much as she didn't want to disturb him—he was dead-asleep, as if he hadn't rested in a long time—panic started to bubble in her chest. Something was wrong. Very wrong. She couldn't remember how she'd gotten here, wherever here was. It was as if she'd been in her apartment one moment and then woken up in an enchanted Nordic castle the next.

But when she called his name, nothing came out except a soft breath of air.

Sam tried again with the same result, and she lifted a hand to her throat out of reflex, surprised to actually find something there. Velvet encircled her entire neck, a collar with no catch or zipper. She picked at the material, scratched at it, but it was glued to her skin.

She dug her fingers deeper and opened her mouth—

*—and the appendage shoved down her throat, filling it until she couldn't breathe, she couldn't move, couldn't scream—*

Strong hands gripped hers, forcing them away from her

throat. Sam pulled her arms tight against her chest and let out a miserable wheezing sound which was nothing like the shout it was supposed to be.

Something pulled her against a warm, solid surface. She couldn't escape its grasp. Davin wouldn't let her go.

Arms trapped, body unable to escape, she fought back in the only way she could.

"Samara, *stop.*"

She froze.

"It's me." A huff of frustration and amusement, familiar. Safe. "Please stop biting."

Sam opened her eyes, and she realized her teeth gripped the thickness of his forearm. She immediately let go.

His expression wasn't pained, and even though she'd bitten down hard, there was no blood, only the imprint of her teeth.

She tried to speak, but his name was silent on her tongue, a question left unvoiced. But she didn't need an answer. It was him. Ash. Not Davin.

She knew that. She'd seen him just a few moments ago. What was wrong with her?

Ash also stared at her with a frown, and his brows folded inward when she pointed at her throat.

"Yeah. That." He winced. "You won't be able to speak for a while. With the injury to your throat, the healers didn't want you to use your voice until it healed. So, they uh, made sure you couldn't."

Her hand went to the collar again, feeling it more closely this time. It was soft and thin, and she should have been able to tear it. She should have been able to speak. What had they done to her?

What had *Davin* done to her?

"You should be able to take it off soon," Ash said, watching her explore the collar. "Two, maybe three days."

Sam pulled her hands away, letting them fall in her lap. Confused, anxious, and now unable to ask anything of relevance. At least if she had her phone, she could type out a message, but she had no idea where it was.

So, she shrugged and spread her hands in the universal sign of *what am I supposed to do?*

"Right, right. Sorry, uh..."

Sam watched him search for something on the nightstand, an ancient wooden piece that looked like it was handmade, the delicate inlaid leaves and vines carved into its corners too detailed for machine work.

"Here."

He handed her a spiral flipbook, along with a black marker. After she took them, Ash returned to the bed, perched on the edge at a more conservative distance away than when he'd held her close to calm her down. Sam could still feel the lingering heat of that closeness, and there was a small amount of regret at his distance. She'd missed her chance to talk to him about Arizona, and now, she would have to wait even longer it seemed.

"Norbu said you might want this in the meantime. I know it's not ideal, but..." He chewed the corner of his lip.

It was jarring to see him without his usual confidence.

When she realized he wasn't going to say anything else, Sam uncapped the marker and wrote her first word on the pad.

**Norboo?**

Sam turned the flipbook and presented it to him.

Ash had lifted his head at the scribbling squeak of her marker, and his troubled expression relaxed into a faint smile. "It's spelled N-o-r-b-u. She's the second-in-command to Lazuli. You might remember him from before when he showed up at your place. They, uh..."

He rubbed the back of his head. "They're...sorcerers."

Sam stared. And stared. And when he didn't crack and let her in on the joke, she wrote another single word and held it up to him.

**What?**

Another shadow of a smile.

"Vates of the Eternal Order. They, well, calling them sorcerers is the easiest comparison to make. But—"

He was interrupted with another scribble.

**Magic?**

Ash winced and said, "If by magic, you mean manipulating energy that exists inside and outside the universe to do their bidding, then yes."

Sam screwed up her face, and the marker pressed indelicately to the page.

**Messing w/ me.**

"I promise I'm not." His smile grew in tandem with her deepening frown. "You've run into three different types of demons, but wizards are where you draw the line?"

Sam blew out her breath, and his smile widened. It wasn't *that* funny, but there was something freeing and commiserating in the gesture, and the shadow left by Davin didn't feel so long and dark.

"I have a lot to tell you," he said as his smile eased. "But I don't know where to begin."

Sam could help with that.

**Where?**

After writing the single word, she pointed at the two of them before gesturing at the room itself. They could be in the center of the Earth or on another planet, for all Sam knew. Lengthy journeys made sense in the nonsensical face of a glowing tear in the world.

But Ash only smiled at the question. "Nowhere, and everywhere. But one of the doorways to this place is only a few minutes away from your apartment. Turns out, if you want to find some wizards, you don't have to look much farther than Downtown Seattle."

The smile faltered the longer Sam stared at him, and he cleared his throat, his tail curling in on itself. It had let go of her wrist after he'd woken up, and she strangely missed its warm pressure.

"Okay, so," Ash began, "these Vates, they essentially act as the vanguard for our world. They protect and guard it from unnatural threats. Such as demons."

A chill straightened Sam's spine, and Ash shifted, as if her disturbance was contagious.

"It's fine," he assured her. "They know what I am. I even help them track and hunt some of the more powerful demons, the rare times we manage to find one. And the Vates are mostly aware of our situation. *Mostly.*"

The emphasis was informative; they didn't know about Sam's mark, and from what little she could recall before she lost consciousness, they didn't know about the feedings either.

His vagueness told her something else too. They might not be free to discuss whatever they wished. Sam didn't know the reason for the secrecy, but she would follow it. She knew Ash, she didn't know the Vates.

*Better the devil you know,* literally.

And then there was the devil she didn't.

Her fingers shook as she wrote out her next question.

**What happened?**

"Your friend was possessed by a heigore."

Sam wrote nothing else. There wasn't much to say without context, but the unfamiliar word crept along her skin.

"They're a type of parasitic demon," Ash said, "a real pain in the ass because they hide in plain sight. The only real giveaway with the bastards is the behavioral changes in their host."

He huffed as if in disbelief or judgement. "They have access to their host's memories and could blend in seamlessly if they wanted. But they're either too stupid or arrogant for subtlety, and it's not hard to expose them through abnormal behavior. Think of the most infamous possessions in history, legend or otherwise, and there's usually a heigore involved. I'm sure you've seen the movies, usually based on the more dramatic cases."

Sam nodded, and Ash continued.

"Surprisingly, the most successful heigore possessions don't involve people, not directly. The heigore will take on an animal host, typically mammalian, and then get close to a human, either through a wild animal attack or through domestication, and infect them that way.

"In fact, the last heigore I met did just that. They can't survive in animal hosts permanently, and this one had an animal host that must have died at some point, because it still controlled its corpse."

Sam went rigid, the soft patter of raindrops in her ears, and soft, wet earth smells invaded her senses.

She wrote again, the lines in uneven strokes.

**Bear?**

Ash stared at her.

"You remember."

Sam wrote again.

**Nightmares.**

"You were fifteen at the time, camping with your mom and uncle," he said, his eyes softening. "I was slow on that one. Too slow. The heigore nearly had you. It was...the second time I had to wipe your memory. I guess it didn't stick then either."

Ash's gaze lost some of its softness.

"Heigore can be intimidating and overdramatic, but it's rare for them to harm their hosts, even during transference. This heigore didn't just rip you with its anchor hooks, it overdosed you with paralytic venom. The Vates said it was either interrupted during the process or forcibly removed. And it wasn't me who did it, I got there after the fact."

He let the silence hang, expectant, but Sam didn't move.

His gaze roamed her face when she neglected to touch the marker to the page.

"Your throat, there was...a lot of damage. You were hemorrhaging." He pressed his lips together hard, his brows dipped in a worried crease. Even his frown lines softened as he spoke. "You could have bled to death. But you didn't, because the venom also acts as a coagulant. As insane as this sounds, it could have been much worse."

*Hands wrapped around her throat from behind, a slithering threat in her ear.*

"I know how hard it is, Samara, but I need you to tell me what happened." His voice was gentle, careful, as he watched her frozen expression. "All of it. Including anything it said to you."

*Demon's whore.*

Sam closed her eyes and shuddered. Davin...the heigore...it had known about her, about the feedings. It had accused her of making a bargain and called Ash her master.

It would have been hard enough to speak aloud; limited to a small notepad would be impossible.

Instead, she scratched out a quick: **Will tell you later.**

Ash's lips pressed into a thin line, but surprisingly, he didn't push.

"Okay. Do you..." He trailed off, grappling for the words. "Is there anything you need?"

Sam knew what he was really asking; he wanted to know if the mark was burning. The mark he'd been so careful to make sure was covered.

Her lips trembled and she shook her head. No, her need was silent, and the mark was inert. What she needed was to curl into a ball under the covers and sleep it off. Maybe when she woke up, she'd be back in her bed, and Davin would still be her overbearing coworker.

At least she knew now why he'd been so interested. Or at least, why the demon using his body as a puppet had been so interested. As it turned out, there was little noticeable difference between a possessive demon and a creep who wouldn't back off.

The temptation of sleep called to her, but first, she had something else to ask.

**Monster?**

Ash's lips twitched into a small smile. "Not sure where he is at the moment, but he's around. I wouldn't worry about him—a wizard's palace is a playground for a beast like him."

Sam frowned at the word *beast,* but it was spoken with something like fondness, so she let it go. Instead, she wrote out another name, the one that twisted her stomach into a nest of knots.

**Davin?**

Ash's smile fell, and it was replaced with an odd blankness.

Even his tail twitched in an unreadable manner as he said, "They're keeping him unconscious. Lazuli wants to make sure his body heals before the exorcism. It'll give him the best chance of survival."

*Exorcism?* That was a real thing? And they were going to attempt one on Davin?

She didn't know how to feel, knowing he hadn't been in control of his actions. His behavior since Halloween was a puzzle she could now solve, the last piece fitting into place.

Davin hadn't been Davin at all, and if he didn't survive the creature inside him, it would be her fault. Sam had been the demon's endgame. Davin had only been a tool, a conduit for him to get there, and she couldn't think about how many other lives might have been ruined in the process.

It was too much. All of it, too much.

"Hey." Ash reached out to her but pulled back before he could touch her. "Your friend is going to be fine. He's relatively young, healthy. Lazuli says his chances are good."

Before he finished speaking, Sam flipped the page to write a new message.

**Coworker.**

Ash frowned. "He was in your apartment. I assumed—"

Sam stared at him, and he sighed.

"It doesn't matter what I assumed. Despite our...situation, you have every right to your own life, to spend it with who you want. It's none of my business who you're intimate with—"

Sam pushed the pad nearly into his face and tapped on the word she had underlined and marked with an exclamation.

**<u>Coworker!</u>**

Ash studied the word and then her face, speaking with careful consideration.

"Heigore often choose their next hosts based on how close they are to the current host. The heigore thought that was you."

Sam's breath stilled. That couldn't be true. It wasn't. What did a stupid parasitic demon know about who Davin cared for? It certainly wasn't Sam. It probably only picked Davin because... because Sam wasn't close to anyone. Not at work, not in her sparse and rare social groups, many of which were solely online. She had no one, not really, so the demon had taken her small crush and twisted it into something perverse.

According to the demon, Sam had always been the target. Davin simply got in the way.

She stared down at her hands, the guilt circling her head like irritating gnats that wouldn't go away. All the unkind thoughts she'd had about him, the way she'd grown to despise and loathe Davin toward the end, she didn't know how to square that. Not when it sat next to the knowledge that he'd been a victim too. Hindsight provided an ugly picture, regardless of the fact she hadn't known the whole truth at the time, and the thing controlling him *did* intend to harm her.

A part of her hoped Davin was unaware the entire time. Not to spare him the suffering of being a prisoner in his own head, but so he wouldn't remember how poorly she'd treated him. And what kind of person did that make her?

The kind of person a demon wanted to possess, apparently.

"Samara?"

Ash spoke her name gently, too gently, and she couldn't meet his eyes. Instead, she wrote across the pad and showed it to him, keeping her gaze fastened on the intricately patterned blankets.

**Why me?**

When he didn't respond, Sam looked up. His lips were

pressed tight together, his brows creased with anxious tension around his eyes.

His voice held that same tension when he spoke. “I mentioned that other demons came through the portal you created, right? The *Alp* was one. This heigore was another. You know about them, because they got the closest. There were more, many more, but they weren’t as cunning or desperate as these two.”

Sam didn’t need to write a word for him to spot the questions in her eyes, and he gave a smile that was closer to an apologetic wince.

“No, I don’t know why they were so keen on you. My guess is it has to do with you being the creator of the portal. The Vates agree, though they never could figure out how you did it. They did a thorough investigation of you, your family, your house in Spokane. They found nothing definitive.”

She frowned at him, and again, he seemed to know exactly what she communicated.

“The Vates know how to blend in, I doubt you even noticed them. I think they showed up to your house as some kind of pest control operation.” He paused, giving her another one of those brittle smiles. “That’s what I was told, anyway. It was around the time they captured me, and I wasn’t exactly in my right mind.”

That brought up a whole basket of other questions, but Ash headed her off before she could start scribbling out demands on her pad. His soft tone, much softer than he usually used with her, was as effective as physically stopping her.

“And I promise to tell you whatever you wish to know. But right now, I should let you rest.”

Ash’s gaze lingered on her right hand, still covered by his glove. He didn’t ask for them back.

"I've stayed too long as it is," he added when Sam remained quiet. "The heigore left a mess behind, and the Vates are going to have their hands full. Things might be a little chaotic for a while, so I'm not sure when I'll be back. Oh, and Lazuli will expect a full debriefing when you're all healed up, so get as much sleep as you can."

He shifted uncomfortably. "And...make sure to keep your hands warm."

*Warm.* Right. She didn't know why they needed to hide it, but Sam could take a guess and say the wizards wouldn't like the idea of these feedings. Or maybe Ash was ashamed. Sam certainly should be.

But...she wasn't. And she wasn't sure when that changed.

Ash stood from the bed.

"Someone should bring you food and new clothing soon. They also request you don't leave the room without an escort." He frowned. "Probably for the best. Easy to get lost in this place, and not everything you meet is friendly."

With that cryptic statement, he turned toward the only door Sam could see, a thick wooden one set into the far wall.

Ash wasn't halfway across the room before Sam's bare feet hit the stone floor, carrying her directly to him, marker and pad left forgotten on the bedspread.

"What—"

He lifted an arm to gesture toward the bed, and Sam slipped underneath it, wrapping her arms tightly around his chest.

She could hear the air escape his lungs as if she'd tackled him instead of hugging him. He was warm, even through the thick fabric of his long-sleeved shirt, and she buried her face in his shoulder. His whole body was a solid mass that kept her grounded, something she needed with a fierceness that took her by surprise.

But it was more than that. Gratitude welled inside her, just as strong as the need for solid ground. If he hadn't shown up when he did, the demon would have killed her.

Ash's hesitation eventually gave way. His arms encircled her with such care, his embrace like a balm for her mind, and there was relief so visceral it left her shaken.

The heigore was wrong. This wasn't slavery or some demonic pact. It was just him. Just Ash. A man who she had once thought was cold, but who only needed to thaw.

"I'm sorry," he said, the words spoken into her hair. "You don't deserve this."

He didn't just mean what the heigore or *Alp* had done. He didn't think she deserved what he did to her, either.

She would have agreed, once, not so long ago. But there were parts of this that weren't terrible. Like right now, when being with Ash made her feel less alone.

To Ash, this was a curse, a horrible thing he did to someone against their will.

To Sam, it was beginning to feel like an excuse for intimacy. And her body thrummed in agreement.

She squeezed her eyes shut. *Not* now, not *now!*

Ash shifted and pulled away, leaving Sam's eyes level with his collarbone and the column of his throat. The mark remained silent, even as her cheeks flushed and her heart pounded too hard.

*Oh. Oh, no.*

Ash cleared his throat. "We'll worry about everything else when this is over, okay?"

So, she wasn't the only one struggling. Was he responding to her desire, or was she responding to his?

Did it matter?

Sam gave a nod and stepped back a safe distance, as if any open space between them could be considered safe. Even as she pulled back, she yearned to rush forward and return to his arms, to safety and warmth and protection from anything that might look her way and bare its teeth.

With a last, lingering look, Ash opened the door. There was a candlelit stone hallway beyond him, and with a heavy click of the door, he was gone.

Sam returned to the bed, setting aside the notepad and marker on the nightstand, and then pulled the cover to her chin. The place held a chill that wasn't unpleasant, but she missed the heat that came with Ash's closeness. She was already looking forward to his return—not just so she could ask about Davin, or because he was familiar in a strange place, but...

She enjoyed being with him. Something had changed after Arizona, and she couldn't pinpoint what it was, but she could pinpoint when it had happened: the long flight home, resting her temple against the thrumming fuselage of the plane, staring out at the clouds below with Ash's low, tempered voice in her ear.

Sam hoped this warmer, more open version of Ash wouldn't withdraw and pull away, not after she'd gotten a glimpse. She wanted to let him in and show him neither of them had to do this alone.

She wanted his closeness, his comfort, his confidence. She wanted... him.

Sam wanted Ash, and it had nothing to do with the feedings.

*Well,* she thought as she stared at the canopy over her head. *Shit.*

***

Thank you for reading! Did you enjoy? Please add your review because nothing helps an author more and encourages readers to take a chance on a book than a review.

And don't miss more in the *Demonic Tendencies* series from L. E. Eyring coming soon!

Until then read THE BINDING STONE, by City Owl Author, Lizzy Gayle. Turn the page for a sneak peek!

Also be sure to sign up for the City Owl Press newsletter to receive notice of all book releases!

# SNEAK PEEK OF THE BINDING STONE

BY LIZZY GAYLE

The magic is palpable. It tingles as it radiates up and down my arms. My eyes snap open the moment I feel it.

I let the power drift over and through me, soaking it up like a human does sunlight. My fingertips crackle with it. Voices become clear now, and sounds assault my ears like daggers after the blissful silence of nothingness. I prefer to sleep. When I do, there is no need to think. Or remember.

Whoever dares disturb my century-long slumber will suffer my wrath. That's a promise.

"Really? Only ten?" The voice of a young man attracts my attention.

He is close, but my senses remain dulled from my sleep inside the gemstone, so I choose to be cautious, staying invisible to human eyes. His voice, warm like honey, soothes the edges of my anger. But some qualities can be deceiving. I know from experience.

"Jer, remind me not to bring you along when I buy a used car," comes the voice of another young man. "Your haggling skills need some serious work."

I stand in the center of a modern marketplace. It is small but cluttered, centered in front of a brick house with several people milling about the lawn and walkways. Whatever time I'm in, the women wear far less clothing than I remember. Near the outskirts of the unkempt grass, I spy a girl who is closest in appearance to me. A small child tugs at her arm, but the woman is distracted. A smile pulls at the corners of my mouth, and I quickly change from the draped fabrics of my last master's time, mirroring her outfit. I nod in approval. I'm going to enjoy this century.

Now to locate and destroy the source of the threat. It is not difficult. I follow the same girl's blushing gaze toward the honeyed voice I'd heard before.

"I'll take it."

He stands a mere table's width from me, and it is clear he is indeed the One. His aura glows like none of the others. A rainbow of iridescent colors pulsates and bleeds around him like a force field. This is too easy.

A gasp draws my attention. It's the young mother, frozen in a state of horror. I've seen that look before, so I follow her stare to find the toddler examining a flower growing in a crack in the concrete. A machine of some sort zooms toward her, so big it will surely crush the child in seconds. Time slows as I raise my fingers and invisible hands lift the young one out of harm's way, setting her securely back near her mother. No one has seen, save the woman who will likely never again be so negligent.

Focusing on the rainbow aura, I raise my hands. All it will take is one blast, directed at the handsome man busy handing a piece of green paper to an elderly woman. He will cease to exist. But I feel it as I let go, and even before it bounces harmlessly off his aura, I know. So I scream. It is not as though anyone can hear it. Not yet.

"Never figured you'd go for the whole bling thing," says the one with glasses and a dull, human aura. "Try it on."

I watch helplessly as Jer slips the ring on his middle finger. The large opal in the center gleams a little too brightly, and I tug at the choker around my neck, running my thumb along the matching stone. I hope the ten-paper is worth more than it appears. Why must I care so much for the innocent after all these years? If I'd let that machine crush the child...

No. I am not, nor will I ever be, one of the human Magicians. It is what sets me apart, and the only thing that may make up for some of my past sins. The ones that were within my control.

"Great. Can we go now please?" It seems by his rush that the friend does not like it here. I cannot blame him. My nose wrinkles up as I scan the rest of the market—a few scattered tables covered in odd objects, dusty boxes stacked and interspersed between them. Most things I don't recognize, but it all looks like junk to me. So how did I end up here? Just one more indignity to add to the list.

I trail behind as the two boys move away and down the wide street. The homes surrounding the market are similar to each other, yet closer together than in my last master's time. It saddens me to find far fewer trees and greenery to balance all the brick and mortar surrounding us as we walk.

The chilled wind carries the ozone-tinted scent and humid feel of a body of water nearby, which pleases me. It is refreshing after my sleep. I let my bare arms stretch out behind me, allowing goose bumps to prickle along my skin. A few buildings away, the men amble up the uneven brick walk, scattering fall's last crisp leaves from the single maple tree in front, before bursting inside the four-story rectangle. I've seen worse. Although I'm certain this "Jer" will be upgrading soon. I continue following them up creaking metal steps and into a small room, containing a sagging, cushioned seat big enough for two, a square table and chairs, a well-worn bed, dresser, and a desk.

"Do you think it's real?" Jer's friend inspects the ring.

"I don't know, Gabe. There was something about it. Like I couldn't put it down."

*Of course not. You sensed the power.* My *power.*

I suppose I should reveal myself. If I do not, the stone will force me, and at least this way I can have a little fun with the friend.

I loosen the invisibility and freeze Jer's friend before he can touch the ring. I will teach him not to touch things that do not belong to him. I grin and let my eyes glow green with power so there can be no doubt as to my nature.

My new master's reaction is immensely satisfying. About to sit in the chair near the desk, he spies me and misses, falling to the floor with a *thud*. His face is pale, his eyes huge as his gaze darts between me and his friend. I would not be surprised if he fainted. Instead, he licks his lips and clears his throat.

"Hel...hello?"

Well, that's different.

---

**Don't miss the next book of the *Demonic Tendencies* series coming soon and find more from L. E. Eyring at leeyring.com**

**Until then, discover THE BINDING STONE, by City Owl Author, Lizzy Gayle.**

**A thousand years of servitude left Leela more than a little jaded. Betrayed by the man she loved only begins her lessons on the wickedness of humanity.**

Her hope for freedom for herself and her fellow Djinn from the magical stones that bind them has dimmed to a barely-there glimmer.

But it hasn't yet been extinguished.

When the young, handsome, and idealistic Jered inadvertently becomes her new master, Leela wonders if his tenderness and concern may be real.

And despite her years of suffering, her heart begins to open to him. And the chance at romance.

As she inches closer to trusting Jered, the past and the enemies that come with it, resurface, threatening the small spark of happiness in Leela's long life.

After a millennium of pain what—and who—is Leela willing to sacrifice for freedom?

Please sign up for the City Owl Press newsletter for chances to win special subscriber-only contests and giveaways as well as receiving information on upcoming releases and special excerpts.

All reviews are **welcome** and **appreciated**. Please consider leaving one on your favorite social media and book buying sites.

Escape Your World. Get Lost in Ours! City Owl Press at www.cityowlpress.com.

# ACKNOWLEDGMENTS

Thank you to my editor, Lisa Green, and the wonderful folks at City Owl Press. You picked me out of a crowd and took a chance on me, and I will never forget that.

I am so grateful to my agent for helping me navigate the new and exciting landscape of publishing. Sara Megibow was always there for me, especially in those inevitable moments of anxiety. With your guidance, it's been more enjoyable and far less treacherous than if I'd embarked on this adventure alone.

I'm eternally lucky to have my supportive friends, my Mom the biggest champion among them. You never doubted me for a second, even when I doubted myself.

And especially, thank you to the wonderful readers I've had over the years, the ones who were there before the publishers and agents. Without you, I wouldn't have dared to dream of such possibilities.

# ABOUT THE AUTHOR

Since the infancy of the internet, L. E. EYRING began her writing journey with a sharpened pencil, a pad of yellow legal paper, and many nonsensical ideas. Those ideas blossomed into a romance with horror, sci-fi, and fantasy, with the need of a good love story hidden amongst the petals. Now, she creates worlds that are equal in beauty and horror, where love can be found in the strangest of hands (or claws, wings, etc.).

A member of the Pacific Northwest Writers Association and the Romance Writers of America, L. E. Eyring is set to make her debut in 2026 with City Owl Press. In her free time when she's not writing "monster romance," she watches educational videos and listens to audio books about nuclear physics, quantum mechanics, and theoretical astrophysics. She resides in Washington state.

leeyring.com

instagram.com/leeyring

bsky.app/profile/leeyring.bsky.social

x.com/LEEyring

pinterest.com/LEEyring

# ABOUT THE PUBLISHER

City Owl Press is a cutting edge indie publishing company, bringing the world of romance and speculative fiction to discerning readers.

Escape Your World. Get Lost in Ours!

www.cityowlpress.com

facebook.com/CityOwlPress

x.com/cityowlpress

instagram.com/cityowlbooks

pinterest.com/cityowlpress

tiktok.com/@cityowlpress

www.ingramcontent.com/pod-product-compliance
Lightning Source LLC
LaVergne TN
LVHW091129080826
845145LV00008B/2097

* 9 7 8 1 6 4 8 9 8 5 6 4 5 *